Praise for Lisa and Laura Roecker

"I was sucked into this series from the very first page, tearing through to the end. So suspenseful, and full of twists and turns!"
—Laurie Faria Stolarz, *New York Times* bestselling author of *Deadly Little Secret*

"No character is above suspicion in this chilling, suspenseful, and smart debut."—*Publishers Weekly*

"[A] smartly paced and plotted first novel, full of twists, clues, and sleuthing. Add this to your go-to list of mysteries."—*Booklist*

"A book for mystery lovers everywhere ... will suck you in and leave you hanging until the very end."
—*RT Book Reviews*

"*The Liar Society* is full of boarding school awesome, secret societies, and misunderstood hot teen boys. It takes a very unique plot for me to enjoy a contemporary YA and *The Liar Society* has unique coming out of the authors' little pink brains."—Bookalicious

THIS IS W.A.R.

lisa roecker & laura roecker

Published in the United States in 2013 by Soho Teen
an imprint of
Soho Press, Inc.
853 Broadway
New York, NY 10003

Library of Congress Cataloging-in-Publication Data

Roecker, Lisa, 1978–
This is W.A.R. / by Lisa and Laura Roecker.
p cm
ISBN 978-1-61695-261-7 (alk. paper)
eISBN 978-1-61695-262-4
1. Murder—Fiction. 2. Vigilantes—Fiction. I. Roecker, Laura.
II. Title. III. Title: This is war.
PZ7.R62515Th 2013
[Fic]—dc23 2013006455

Interior design by Janine Agro, Soho Press, Inc.

Printed in the United States of America

10 9 8 7 6 5 4 3 2 1

To Michael Roecker for teaching us that girls can do anything and everything that boys can do. Usually better.

THIS IS W.A.R.

July 4th, 11:32 P.M.

Willa Ames-Rowan never thought she would die. She firmly believed white should be worn before Labor Day, champagne was best enjoyed on an empty stomach, and sleep was for the weak. If it weren't for the inky black water tugging at her limbs, clawing its way into her mouth, she might have welcomed the dark solitude of Hawthorne Lake. She might have floated on her back, counting stars, dreaming about what it would be like to wake up next to her future husband. What it might be like to marry James Gregory.

But not tonight.

Tonight, Willa Ames-Rowan was drowning.

As luck would have it, she'd just read an article recounting a tsunami survivor's near-death experience in a tattered copy of Reader's Digest *while waiting for her acupuncture appointment earlier in the week. Willa took comfort in the survivor's story because just before he passed out from lack of oxygen, he felt a moment of peace. He gave himself to the water, accepted his fate.*

So Willa knew she couldn't be dying because there was nothing peaceful about her struggle to determine which way was up, down, left, or right. The moment she went under, she'd decided to decline death's invitation—with the socially acceptable level of regret, of course. She knew enough to remain calm, tread water, back float until someone noticed she was missing. Contrary to her sister's judgy texts, Willa was a fighter. She would never let her life slip away in a Hallmark movie moment of blissful surrender.

She'd only had a couple of drinks, but her head was cloudy and her limbs sluggish and heavy. She'd been raised on the water—boating trips, beach vacations, the Club pool—she should have been above the surface, not under it. Earlier in the afternoon, Willa had taken a dip in this very same water while the girls lounged on the beach. Madge had yelled at her not to swim out too far, brown hair swirling around her face in the wind, her fair skin shielded by layers of sunscreen and a long, gauzy cover-up. Next to her, Lina was burying her nose in a magazine, all boobs and legs, doing her best impression of not giving a shit. And then there was Sloane with her pin-straight hair and black almond eyes, looking like a tiny beacon in her bright pink bikini. She stood next to Madge, shielding the sun with her hand. Even from the distance, Willa could see the smile tugging at her lips. If Sloane weren't so self-conscious, she might have been cheering.

And so it was her friend's silent encouragement that pushed Willa on as brief bursts of light shone in the dark sky overhead, fireworks guiding her toward the surface. She scissored her legs toward the red, white, and blue explosions.

Her lungs burned, the muscles of her arms wept for a break. But still, she fought.

Images of the Gregory brothers bubbled to the surface of her consciousness. She couldn't think of them now. She couldn't think of the look on Rose McCaan's face when Rose saw her kissing James Gregory.

Willa knew Rose had a thing for James Gregory.

She knew but she didn't care, and now she couldn't help but wonder if that kiss had somehow landed her here in this water. Willa would take it back if she could. She'd take a lot of things back. And for a moment she thought she might actually have the chance. She finally broke free of the lake's slippery grip. Her head bobbed into the cool night air. But she opened her mouth too early and choked on the stagnant water. Hacking and sputtering, she was able to keep her head up long enough to drink in gasps of oxygen between coughs. The agony in her lungs slowly faded, and for the briefest of moments, she thought she was going to live to write a much more accurate drowning survival story, preferably for Teen Vogue.

Willa never saw the hands that pushed her head back under.

She never felt the water fill her lungs.

And she was completely unaware of the champion-sized trout grazing her lifeless arm.

Willa Ames-Rowan never gave up and welcomed death.

Willa Ames-Rowan simply died.

PART 1

S.A.R. (Search and Rescue)

Chapter 1

Rose stared at the water and whispered the Hail Mary in Spanish, the way her grandmother had taught her. She wasn't sure if she believed in God, at least not the one the nuns at St. Agnes ranted and raved about, but Mary was a different story. Every summer she'd spent with her grandmother, she'd been reminded that Mary watched out for good little girls, especially good little girls with the middle name Marie. And something about the way her grandmother clutched the Rosary to her chest, blue beads tinkling against the silver cross, her knuckles white beneath papery skin, had always made Rose want to believe.

The repetition calmed her. She understood why people prayed in the face of tragedy. Praying provided the illusion of control. And of course, there was the niggling possibility that the prayer might actually work. A miracle like the ones her grandmother had read to her from the back pages of Spanish tabloid magazines.

Rose shivered in spite of the humid air. It looked like every member of Hawthorne Lake Country Club was on the beach. The women stood in tight circles, whispering and crying, while their husbands rushed around trying to look useful. Their movements seemed designed to look important. If they walked with enough authority and spoke in quiet, reassuring tones, they might be able to bring Willa Ames-Rowan back to life.

But it was all a lie. Like everything else at Hawthorne Lake.

Willa was dead. The ambulance had screamed off in a blaze of sirens twenty minutes ago. Even in the darkness, Rose saw the blue of Willa's lips and the way her arm dangled off the side of the stretcher before it was gently placed back at her side. Now there was nothing left to do but pray to her grandmother's Mary.

"Rose! Thank the lord." Her mom wrapped her thin arms around Rose's body and squeezed too hard. "I've been looking for you everywhere." She was dressed like all of the other women on the beach that night, but with her jet-black eyes and café au lait skin, she might as well have been wearing a Club worker's uniform. As Hawthorne Lake's event planner, Pilar McCaan was afforded most of the same privileges as members, but she was still considered "staff" by everyone who mattered. Despite her efforts to suppress it, the accent that snuck its way into a handful of her words didn't help.

Rose stiffened in her mom's arms. She wanted to forget everything she'd seen over the course of the night. To un-know all the secrets. But she had watched Willa stumble around the yacht. And she'd seen her mom navigate the party as if social climbing were an extreme sport. The past six hours ran on repeat in her brain like some kind of terrible movie. But there was no director calling scenes or strategically fading to black when images grew too intense. No Oscar award-winning makeup artist had perfected the blue of Willa's lips or added silicone strips to mimic the bloating of her skin.

Every moment was real. And it was all burned in high-definition into Rose's memory.

"Are you okay?" Rose's mom held her at arm's length, her thick-lashed eyes probing her daughter's. "Did you see? I mean, I can't believe she's . . . You can't tell him." Her mom was using the voice she reserved for male members when their hands wandered a little too low at one of the Club's famous star-lit parties. Rose always thought of it as her business voice, and it normally stopped her dead in her tracks. But tonight she just shrugged her mom's hands off her shoulders and resumed her vigil, her lips moving, the sound trapped inside.

Dios te salve, María, llena eres de gracia . . .

"He's going to ask you questions. You have to be prepared to answer them." White shone around the black of her mom's wide eyes. "You know what will happen if you tell him the truth," she whispered.

Rose nodded, her eyes fixed on the black and blue expanse of water in front of her. As the sky lightened on the cusp of morning, the color resembled an angry bruise.

Santa María, Madre de Dios . . .

Rose had lived the first seventeen years of her life without ever having made a mistake. Well, unless you counted the time she'd let Katelyn Norris copy her English homework on the bus to school and was too afraid to speak up when her teacher questioned the identical paragraphs.

Her mom's short, square nails dug into her Rose's flesh as they wove their way through the small groups of members still scattered across the beach. Rose regretted wearing sandals that pinched her toes, the heels sinking into the sand, slipping with every step. How stupid she'd been standing in front of her closet, pushing her feet into different shoes, yanking shirt after shirt over her head, and leaving the rejects heaped in a corner. She'd never cared before. Tonight she cared too much. Maybe *that* was her first mistake.

No. She knew better.

Her first mistake had come long before criticizing her reflection in the mirror. It was the moment she'd accepted James Gregory's invitation to his family's annual Fourth of July party. Or maybe it went even farther back, to the moment he caught her hiding in the boathouse, the night of the Club's Summer Swing.

Rose shook her head slightly, her mouth still moving through the prayer. None of it mattered. Pinpointing the exact moment everything began to fall apart wasn't going to change a thing.

And yet . . . maybe it was her last mistake that really counted: the moment her dad had swung her off the yacht, his detective's badge catching the moonlight.

"Rose, what happened? Did you see anything?" His voice had probably sounded calm and professional to the perfectly coiffed couple standing behind her, but Rose could hear the note of panic underlining every word like a silent exclamation mark. Her dad had been around long enough to know that accidents didn't happen at Hawthorne Lake. Rose had started to respond but choked on her words when she saw the paramedics frantically pumping Willa's chest on the beach directly behind her dad. She had watched as they finally gave up and wheeled her slowly toward the truck.

"I have no idea what happened."

Out of all the mistakes she'd made that night, this was the one she regretted the most.

Her mom yanked hard on her arm, pulling her through the crowd of people standing around the parking lot. Rose stared blankly at their old Lexus. It seemed wrong for it to be there. Normal, unchanged after everything that had happened tonight. She finished the prayer in English, the words barely a whisper.

Pray for us sinners,
Now and at the hour of our death.

To her surprise, before her mom unlocked the door, she met Rose's dark eyes with her own and whispered, "Amen."

Chapter 2

It was strange to see Carolina Winthrop cry. Rose had known her since they were little, not that Lina had ever acknowledged her existence. The tears looked out of place on Lina's heavily made-up face, like rain in the desert. Her shoulders hunched over, the deep-V falling along the back of her shirt revealing the requisite Chinese character tattoo. (It probably translated into something like: "poor little rich girl with serious daddy issues.") Her black bra strap fell off her shoulder and hung loosely over her upper arm, also covered in intricate inked designs.

Lina was made up of jagged angles and hard lines, all pointy elbows and razor-sharp cheekbones. Everything about Lina—from her aggressively short, bleached-blonde hair to her infamous eyebrows cocked in permanent judgment—screamed *bitch*.

Rose's mom sighed and shook her head as she watched her husband comfort the girl.

"Unbelievable. She knows, but she'll never tell. It's a good thing your father's a terrible cop." There was grim satisfaction in her mom's voice.

Rose hated herself for feeling the same skepticism that radiated off her mom. On one hand, she wanted, needed Lina to keep Willa's death a secret. Rose had lied to her dad for reasons she couldn't even bring herself to think about. Reasons that were tied up in late nights spent on the beach with James Gregory. Her mind flashed back to his dark blonde hair, the way his lips had felt on hers, the way his fingers left a trail of electricity behind as they slid underneath her shirt. She'd trusted him with her secrets and maybe even a tiny piece of her heart. How could she have been so wrong about him? How could she have given herself so completely to someone who was capable of something so awful?

Rose and Lina and pretty much every single person on the damn boat knew who had killed Willa that night. But even with a yacht full of witnesses, her dad would never hear the truth. Not even from his own daughter, not from one of Willa's best friends, and especially not from his wife.

Rose flung open the door and sat on the curb in front of the car. It wasn't much cooler outside, but at least she wouldn't have to be trapped with her mom. Thankfully the gently lapping water made it impossible for her to hear the conversation between Lina and her dad. She didn't trust herself to listen to all the lies. If she heard enough, the truth might just come spilling out.

Mari Jacobs plopped down next to Rose on the curb.

"Five thousand dollars." Her voice was flat.

Rose didn't need to ask Mari what she meant. She knew that was the money she'd been offered by the Gregory family to keep quiet, and she knew Mari had taken it. No one turned down a bribe from the Gregorys, especially not a waitress putting herself through college.

For a minute Rose looked into Mari's dark brown eyes, took in her perfect heart-shaped face and coconut-colored skin. It drove Rose's mom insane that she spent so much time talking to "the help" instead of hanging out with kids her own age. Never mind that Mari read actual books and was funny as hell. Rose had far more in common with Mari than she did with girls like Lina Winthrop. As the daughter of a cop and Hawthorne Lake's event planner, Rose was treated with the same faux respect reserved for crossing guards and doormen. She looked at her dad, scribbling on a tiny notebook with his favorite chewed up pen, while Lina Winthrop sobbed out lie after lie.

Joe McCaan was of average height, average build, and if Rose was being completely honest, slightly below-average intellect. That's not to say that her dad was dumb; he was just the kind of man who always saw the best in people. A great quality for a dad, not the best quality for a detective.

Her mom was a different story, of course. As one of the highest-ranking employees at the Club, it was Pilar McCaan's job to see everything and know everyone. Club employees were terrified of her while most members ignored her completely. Like the new curtains that hung in the grand foyer: she was too gauche and shiny to match the rest of the Club, but too bothersome to replace. As Pilar's daughter, Rose fit the same bill. There were only three people who seemed to ignore her dubious pedigree. One of them was Mari Jacobs. The other was James Gregory. The last person was dead.

Mari's hand shook a little as she reached into her bag and pulled out a cigarette. "Same price they were offering last summer. You'd think they'd at least adjust for inflation."

Normally Rose would have laughed. Instead she kept staring at her dad and Lina. Rose watched Lina's black-rimmed eyes wander, heard all the words that weren't being said. And even though she'd done the same thing, had spoken the same lie aloud, watching one of Willa's best friends slowly shake her head back and forth made her hate Lina Winthrop even more than she already did.

Mari blew a cloud of smoke through puckered lips.

Rose could feel her eyes. She wanted her to talk, to say something.

"I'm so sick of this shit, I really am. James Gregory goes off and kills the Club princess, and the best Gramps can do is offer up five Gs?" Mari paused. "I'm over it. I'm sick of taking bribes that barely cover the cost of books."

Rose couldn't bring herself to look at Mari. She wasn't in the mood for one of their epic discussions about the caste system of the Club. Not now.

"You think Lina's parents are here?"

Mari scanned the crowd lazily, but Rose knew the answer to her own question. The Winthrops wouldn't be there waiting to comfort Lina after the traumatic questioning was over. They were probably off on another one of their lavish vacations.

Harsh stripes of mascara stained Lina's cheeks as she turned around and gestured to Sloane Liu. Sloane wiped her eyes with the back of her hand and walked forward, wisps of her hair lifted by the breeze off the lake. She wore a pale-pink, silky dress, the hem fluttering. If the circumstances weren't quite so tragic, she might have looked beautiful.

As soon as she began speaking, she broke down, her head in her hands.

"Wow, she really knows how to turn on the waterworks."

Mari ground her cigarette into the asphalt of the parking lot and shook her head slowly.

Rose felt a rush of jealousy. Sloane's parents enveloped their tiny daughter in an effort to protect her from the big bad detective, who stood there looking like he might start crying himself. It must be nice to be so loved. After a few awkward minutes spent shuffling around and looking at his watch, Detective McCaan tried questioning Sloane again, but her parents shook their heads, silent understanding passing from parent to parent.

Rose had to look away while her dad dug business cards out of his wallet and handed them to Lina and Sloane. She had heard him say the words so many times in the past that she was able to recite them out loud for Mari's benefit.

"Call me if you think of anything that might help the investigation. Or even if you just feel like talking about what happened tonight. Part of my job is to be here for the community." She even managed a passable imitation of her dad's honest, sympathetic, guileless smile—the one that always flickered across his face while he let yet another crime go unpunished.

"You've got it down, my friend. Maybe you should apply for deputy." Mari laughed. It sounded more to Rose like she was choking.

Rose stood up and brushed the sand off the backs of her thighs. Her dad would probably be here all morning tying up loose ends. For him there was no crime scene to worry about, just a tragic accident that would be handled with the utmost discretion.

Her mom was watching impatiently from the driver's seat. As much as Rose hated the thought of getting back into the car with her, at least she got to go home. Now that the police were wrapping up on the boat, crowds of people began to pull away. A sliver of bright orange appeared along the horizon, the sky surrounding pink with the promise of a new day. Everything looked different in the rising light; dresses appeared out of place, heavily made-up faces seemed completely inappropriate. She tugged at the silky fabric that seemed too short to be a dress in the light of day. Motors turned over, car doors opened and shut; people pulled away to begin the process of forgetting.

"See you tomorrow, I guess." Rose started walking toward her mom's car when she heard Mari's voice call out to her.

"I didn't take it."

She froze mid-step, blood pulsing in her skull. *No, no, no. Mari couldn't have turned down the Gregorys' money. No one turned down the Gregorys.*

"But . . . your job, your apartment, what are you going to do?" Rose asked, turning.

"Don't worry. I've got a plan." Mari flashed a crooked smile. "Not that it matters to you. I saw what you were up to last night."

"But it's the Gregorys," Rose continued, ignoring the way her stomach clenched. Mari always had an angle, a way out of any situation. But she was out of her league with the Gregorys, and they both knew it.

Now that she'd practically spit in the Gregorys' faces, there was no way she'd last the rest of the summer. Saying "no" to the Gregorys meant her job would be mysteriously downsized; a gas leak or a termite infestation would leave the tiny apartment she'd rented for the summer uninhabitable. Typewritten threats, sent via envelopes with no return address, would ensure that she left town quickly and quietly. Mari knew all of this, but still she'd turned down their

money. Rose felt sick as she remembered the bitter taste of
the lie she'd told her dad. She was a coward. She hated herself for it. Even worse, she saw that same disgust mirrored
in Mari's flinty eyes.

So Rose said nothing to her friend. Instead she climbed
into her mom's car and focused on the sun rising up over the
lake. A slender, dark-haired girl stood by the edge of the water.
The rising sun bounced off her porcelain skin like a spotlight,
announcing Madge Ames-Rowan, the star of the tragic show.
It seemed odd for her to be there instead of at the hospital
with her family. Madge was Willa's stepsister. Their parents
had married when they were in kindergarten, and they'd been
best friends ever since. Together they bookended the teen social
scene at the Club. Rose was almost scared to look at her,
afraid that the grief would be too raw, that it would burn and
leave a scar.

But there were no tears on Madge's face.

Rose saw only fury and a steely determination. Madge's
fingers were at her neck, twisting the small key she always
wore, her green eyes trained on the Gregorys' yacht that
bobbed and swayed in its slip. When Rose followed Madge's
gaze, she met their target. The Gregorys. James was sprawled
out in one of the lounge chairs on the deck. Trip sat next to
him, cradling his mop of red curls in his hands. If the twins
were crowned princes of the Club, their grandfather, Charles
"the Captain" Gregory, was king. The Captain ruled with a
platinum fist, and now he paced the perimeter of the deck, his
back ramrod straight, chin tilted toward the lightening sky.
Another battle won.

Willa had only been dead for a few hours and her killer
was passed out in a lounge chair. His grandfather had
begun the process of paying for his innocence. Rose knew

right then that Willa's stepsister wasn't mourning. She was plotting.

Madge and the Captain knew what everybody else at that party knew: Willa hadn't fallen off the yacht in a drunken stupor. She'd gotten into a motorboat with James Gregory. An hour later he'd returned alone, his blond hair dark with lake water. And they had all lied about what they saw that night when the police finally pulled Willa's body out of the lake.

Of course they had. That was the rule. That was the thing about Hawthorne Lake.

The most important rule wasn't a part of the ridiculous bylaws the Captain wrote in the new member orientation packet. Sure, members got a slap on the wrist if they were caught wearing pink on the tennis courts or if they allowed a woman in the gentlemen-only quarters. But there was only one unbreakable rule at the Club. No one dared even say it out loud. It was the kind of rule that could be communicated in harsh glances, quiet resignations, and abrupt disappearances. It was the kind of rule that meant when you saw one of the Gregory twins take a girl out on the lake and return alone, you kept your mouth shut. (And if that didn't work, it meant you suddenly started talking about how many martinis the girl drank and how rough the water was that night.) It was the kind of rule that meant that if you turned down the Gregorys' hush money, you better get the hell out of Hawthorne Lake. Because if you were handsome enough and if you were rich enough, it was the kind of rule that let you get away with murder.

Chapter 3

"Rose! Come on! We're going to be late!"

Rose made her way to the garage, her eyes bloodshot and burning after another sleepless night.

It had been three weeks since Willa Ames-Rowan's ashes had been scattered into the lake. Three weeks of staff gossip, socialite whispers, and the intense mourning limited to Willa's inner circle. Three weeks since Mari had stopped returning any of Rose's texts, claiming that she needed to focus on work if she were going to keep her job. But Rose knew the truth. Rose had chosen her side when she'd lied to her dad; Mari had chosen hers when she turned down the Gregorys' money.

Esteemed members of the Hawthorne Lake Country Club handled the tragedy much like they handled rare bone cancers and childhood diseases with no cure: they threw money at it. Within days of Willa's death, a scholarship fund was established and was rumored to have enough money in it to send an entire class of inner city kids to an Ivy League college.

Donations were encouraged in lieu of flowers. Members quickly latched onto the opportunity to absolve themselves of whatever guilt they felt. Rose imagined them carefully writing checks, lifting the corner of one of the ornate rugs in the game room and sweeping the entire mess underneath it. The truth was, aside from a noticeable quiet, not much had changed. Except, of course, that she had nobody now, with Mari dead to her and Willa . . . dead to everyone.

Rose had seen a single calla lily left by the dock early one morning, but by the time she returned for lunch, it was gone. No doubt, any other small tributes were all promptly removed by a well-trained employee.

A week after Willa died, Rose had cut out the front-page article in the *Hawthorne Times* and tucked it between the pages of her journal. She hadn't been able to write about what happened that night. The picture of Willa with her blue eyes, blonde hair, and the long list of lies detailing her final hours would serve as a reminder. Rose wasn't trying to forget. She was punishing herself by remembering. She'd tucked the journal in her underwear drawer beside the Virgin Mary figurine her grandmother had given her when she had turned thirteen. Fitting.

"Rose! Let's go!" Her mom waited impatiently by the door in a suit that was two inches too short to be considered classy. She reached over and tucked one of Rose's curls behind her ear. "I'm doing this for you, you know. You might not realize it yet, but surrounding yourself with people of this caliber . . . it's a gift."

"More like a curse." Rose jerked out of her mom's reach. She wanted to scream out all of the secrets that she had so carefully buried. But they died one by one before they even reached her tongue.

"Careful, Rose." Her mom's eyes flashed. "You can spend the day at the bar with Mari if you want. Just get in the car."

It was ironic; if Mari had been angry with her before everything changed, Rose probably would have sought out Willa. Not that she'd been a friend. Not really. But she had talked to her occasionally. Treated her like an actual person instead of a piece of furniture you had to step around to get to the pool. The kind of person who could make someone's day better just by smiling. She always had a smile for everyone at the Club, but when she smiled at *you*, it felt different, personal. Like she was genuinely happy to see you.

Rose would never forget her first day at the Club. The sea of slit eyes following the small, light brown-skinned girl from the pool to the lake: ignored by all of the members, forgotten by her mother, avoided by the staff. She hid behind her romance novels and pretended not to care. But that same morning, Willa returned from summer camp. She caught Rose hiding behind the boathouse and tried to convince her to come hang out with the other girls—Madge, Lina, and Sloane—gathered on a blanket on the beach. Rose was so flustered she could barely force herself to shake her head no in response. It would have been social suicide. She would have been the laughingstock of the Club. And Willa must have known because the next morning there was a new book by her favorite author waiting for her behind the boathouse. It was an offer of friendship Rose never quite mustered up the courage to acknowledge.

And now . . . well, now Rose was able to see Hawthorne Lake for what it was. And she hated it.

She couldn't blame Mari for shutting her out. Mari had worked at the Club for the past two summers—and somewhere between dodging stoner busboy Rory O'Neil's advances and modeling designer sunglasses rescued from the lost and found, they'd become friends. Rose had begged her mom to let her waitress with Mari, but there was no way Pilar McCaan was going to let her only daughter walk around the Club in a uniform. Her mom insisted that Rose take full advantage of the privileges afforded her and use them to network.

Rose had different ideas. She preferred to lurk on the outskirts of the Club's employee social scene, eavesdropping on college-aged servers who spent most of their time bitching and moaning about the very same people Rose was supposed to be infiltrating. When Mari was around, they had almost accepted her.

Now she was back in no man's land. Not a member. Not an employee. A nobody.

Rose didn't even bother saying goodbye to her mom before she headed to the sunroom with her bag of library books. The sunroom was one of Rose's favorite places at the Club. Huge glass windows overlooked the pool, the golf course, and the grounds beyond. Light filtered in through panes of glass in long stripes, illuminating the dust in the air with a sort of timeworn sparkle. It was the perfect place for people watching, an art Rose had perfected long ago. She wasn't allowed to sit at the tables along the perimeter that were reserved for actual members, but she spent hours sitting at the bar, a book in her lap like an alibi. Rose was still hopeful that if she hung around long enough, Mari would eventually decide to start talking to her again. She tried not to let her disappointment show when Hannah's head popped up from under the long expanse of mahogany.

"You shouldn't be here," Hannah hissed.

"Where's Mari?" For one panicked second, Rose was sure that she'd been fired . . . or worse.

"Don't worry about her, she's just fine." Hannah never smiled unless someone was doing something they shouldn't. But Rose didn't bother asking her for details. Hannah, like most of the staff at Hawthorne, didn't give a shit about Pilar's careful instructions to avoid socializing with her daughter. She just resented Rose for being able to laze around Hawthorne Lake all day while she served drunk golfers and anorexic housewives. But Rose had found that sometimes if she sat at the bar long enough, Hannah's boredom would eventually win out, and she'd start talking.

"I can't believe they're out there working on their tan after everything that happened," Rose offered.

Hannah followed Rose's gaze. Lina, Sloane, and Madge sat along the pool edge, their legs dangling into the water. The group looked off balance without Willa, an odd instead of an even. Madge's green eyes were blank. The gold key around her neck hung limply in the sunlight. Sloane had folded her tiny body in half and looked seconds away from bursting into tears. Lina hunched over, fidgeting with the strap of her string bikini, a bandage on the inside of her wrist. Probably a fresh tattoo. "Willa was always the nice one," Hannah said. She shook her head slowly, never taking her eyes off the girls.

Rose didn't bother reminding Hannah that she used to refer to Willa as "Queen Bitch" because she always insisted on ordering her salad dressing on the side. Death has a knack for photoshopping memories. She thought back to the beginning of the summer. Had her own memories been photoshopped too? She remembered the time she'd been hiding out under her favorite tree on the grounds, tearing through another trashy romance novel. The second she saw Willa approach she packed up her book and stood to leave. Willa's obvious crush on the Club's heir apparent was no secret and rumor had it James Gregory was finally starting to warm up. So she tucked her head into her chest and barreled toward the clubhouse.

But Willa stopped her and grabbed the paperback out of her hand. "McNaught, huh? Have you read any Garwood? She's got the best manhood euphemisms."

Rose could only blink heavily in response. If blinking out phrases in Morse code were a socially acceptable form of conversation, she would have been Homecoming Queen. She wasn't sure what shocked her more, the fact that Willa truly did love trashy romance as much as she did or that Willa had correctly used an SAT word in a sentence.

"Judith Krantz is actually my favorite?" Rose had that terrible habit of transforming statements into questions when she was nervous.

"Ah, *Scruples*! I've been trying to get Madge to read that, but she can't get past all the nasty eighties hair."

They'd spent the next half hour rating romance novels based on overall sexiness and bad fashion decisions. Rose figured it would be the highlight of her summer. Little did she know . . .

"You hear the latest about James?" Hannah asked, jerking Rose from her memories.

Rose's stomach dropped. Instead of waiting for a response, Hannah sighed heavily and pushed out from behind the bar. She set the salads down carefully in front of a table of women still in tennis whites. Not one of them acknowledged her presence. Hawthorne Lake's menu was heavy on steak and almost completely devoid of what Rose's mom always referred to as "chick food." Thankfully most of the women at the Club didn't eat in public, so it didn't really matter if they had to order the same wilted side salad every single day. Lunch went as ignored as the staff.

Once Hannah had again settled behind the bar, she raised her eyebrows. "So? James? Anything?"

"Yeah . . ." The napkin Rose had been twisting in her lap tore in half, and she looked up into Hannah's light, watery eyes. "I heard that the Captain sent him away. Some military school or whatever?"

"You heard wrong," she whispered. "James and the Captain are back to their weekly golf game. Apparently enough time has passed for *that* to start again."

Rose blinked. Ever since James could walk he'd been playing golf each week with his grandfather, so it made sense. Besides, the Captain *was* his legal guardian. She always had to remind herself that James and Trip had no real parents: a tragic car accident had left them—the Captain's daughter and her husband—dead. But she still had to resist the temptation to shiver, gag, or worse. It was too soon, too soon . . .

"And get this," Hannah leaned closer to Rose, close enough for her to catch a hint of vanilla lotion. "The valets parked a brand-new BMW. James's brand-new BMW. Apparently Trip got the old one."

Hannah's voice dripped with scorn. But she wasn't fooling anyone. Rose knew if either of the Gregory boys offered Hannah a ride, she'd melt. And Rose couldn't blame her. She had the same reaction to them. Everyone at the Club did. You hated them until they threw you that little scrap of hope. Then all bets were off.

Her face flushed at the thought of James in his brand-new car. If she hadn't destroyed the napkin in her lap, she could have wiped the beads of sweat gathering above her lip. James was definitely the favored grandson, but Trip seemed pretty content with his brother's hand-me-downs. Of course, Rose imagined that if *her* sloppy seconds consisted of a BMW 3 series with a few thousand miles on it, she'd probably be pretty happy herself.

While Hannah jabbered on about the many features and upgrades in James's new car, Rose couldn't help but wonder which Gregory had offered Mari $5,000 to keep her mouth shut. The Captain himself? Or maybe it was Trip who was forced to do the dirty deed. She lifted her glass of water to her lips with shaking hands, and the nausea passed. No, it was probably James. Rose could imagine Mari turning him down, especially if he were drunk. He'd been fully sauced that night, after all. God only knew what he'd done to Willa on that little boat . . .

She cringed inwardly at the time she'd spent with him. Whispers in dark corners of the Club, meaningful glances exchanged over the pool. She had been so sure that he was different. That he was real.

"How can he even show his face?" Hannah asked as though she expected Rose to provide her with an acceptable answer.

She leaned over the bar, eyes narrowed toward the pool. For a second Rose thought she might know something, but then the girl took a step back and frowned. The closest Hannah ever got to an apology. Rose followed her eyes out the wall of windows to the pool deck. The sparkling water lay still, the only evidence the girls had been there was a trail of wet footprints along the surrounding stone.

"I guess it's easy when you're a Gregory?" Rose finally responded.

The words were barely out of her mouth before the carefully modulated hum of lunch was shattered by the sound of breaking glass.

Chapter 4

All heads in the sunroom turned. Tanned necks stretched past the bar. A couple of ancient plastic surgery casualties even managed to raise an eyebrow. Rose swiveled toward the door just in time to see Madge in a kelly-green maxi dress, pool bag slung over her shoulder. Her eyes were fixed on Trip Gregory, while Lina and Sloane stood frozen behind her.

Trip had the decency to avert his eyes as he passed the girls and strode through the room. But his gaze flickered toward Rose for the briefest of moments, setting her entire body on fire. Her secret, *their secret,* was a target on her chest. It killed all the parts of her that were still alive.

By the time he made it to a lounge chair outside, throwing his long body onto it, Rose almost relaxed. But the sunroom was still frozen. Because Trip hadn't been the one to break the glass; his drunken brother had. Rose felt the heat of eyes on her neck but kept her gaze trained on her lap. She knew exactly who was looking at her, but she was terrified of what her eyes would say if she looked back. Curiosity eventually got the best of her. James swayed by the door using the frame to balance. He didn't look at Madge or even acknowledge her friends. Instead he focused intently on Rose.

She looked away, praying Hannah didn't notice him staring. Her heart thudded. Meanwhile, Madge stood her ground as every member and employee waited for her to react. Even from her perch at the bar, Rose could feel the tension. Lina leaned over and whispered something in Madge's ear, bleached hair grazing freckled cheek. But Madge shook Lina's arm from her shoulder and stood in the doorway like she was preparing to pounce. Rose allowed herself another quick glance at James. Her dark eyes met his blue, and she felt the familiar rush of heat. Like muscle memory, her body remembered what it was like to be close to his, and it reacted.

"*You.*"

The spell was broken. Madge hissed the word so quietly Rose almost thought she'd imagined it. Bunny Westinghouse, one of Mrs. Ames-Rowan's oldest friends, must have sensed imminent disaster because she was out of her seat and at Madge's side before James could even respond.

"I'm so sorry. This young lady is going through a very difficult time." Bunny used her spindly arms to carefully guide Madge over the broken glass and away from James. She shot darts with her eyes at Hannah as though saying, *"Fix this."* Hannah rushed to the door to fulfill her duty.

But before Rose could escape, James was there. Next to her. Impossible to ignore. He reeked of vodka, sweat, and desperation. Rose hadn't noticed from across the bar, but his eyes were rimmed with purple circles. The wry laughter she'd seen dance there was gone. It was all bleary redness.

"I . . ." Before he could continue, Rose jumped to her feet and flew to Hannah's side. Helping Hannah clean up the broken glass seemed like her best option. But when she reached for a shard of glass the edge sliced her finger. Blood rushed to the surface before the pain even registered.

James appeared with a towel.

"You should watch yourself, Rose." He stumbled a little, his lips twisted into an unstable smile. "I'm dangerous, you know."

He reached for her, and Rose jerked her arm away, a drop of blood falling to the floor. Her stomach churned. She was 99% sure she'd throw up if he touched her. Luckily he just tossed her the towel and laughed when it landed on top of the broken shards.

The James that she had known all summer was gone. Or maybe he'd never really existed at all. She would never admit it to Mari or even herself, but when she had lied to her dad the night of Willa's death, she had lied for James. Holding the towel to her finger, she couldn't deny the facts any longer. She couldn't pretend that the asshole staggering around the sunroom was innocent. When James stumbled past the table Madge, Lina, and Sloane now shared with Mrs. Westinghouse, Rose held her breath again. Everyone did.

Even though he was a drunken murderer, James Gregory was still the crowned prince of Hawthorne Lake. If one of the girls made a move, life as they knew it would end.

Rose waited, silently hoping one of them would race forward, claw at his jugular, tear at his heart. She wondered if grief could make a person brave. All three of them sat perfectly still. Anger and righteous indignation bubbled up in Rose's chest. How could they sit there and tolerate a guy who should be in jail? They were *smiling*, even.

But when she looked closely at Madge, the towel around her finger darkening with blood, Rose realized the smile never made it to her eyes. And then—so fast that if Rose had blinked a second earlier she might have missed it—Madge nodded sharply at Lina and Sloane. The girls' smiles broadened ever so slightly in return.

Chapter 5

The dated locker room was one of the few places in the Club where Rose felt comfortable. At least she could be alone there. Surrounded by faded pink floral wallpaper and the yellowing Formica countertops, Rose's heartbeat slowed. The women of the Club were constantly petitioning for a renovation, but there was never money left in the budget after golf course repairs, new meeting room accommodations, and the countless upgrades to the men's locker room. Muzak played softly in the background, and the air was heavy with the scent of potpourri. She hadn't realized how much the morning—or if she were being honest, James's presence—had shaken her. She needed time to think.

She did a quick sweep of the locker room. When she was sure she was alone, she slipped through a hidden door into the laundry room. Technically, the employees-only parts of the Club were off-limits to Rose, but the laundress always took a late lunch. Lately, the rhythmic beating of the washers and dryers was the only noise that could drown out all the voices in her head.

The tension in her shoulders eased as she threw herself on top of a pile of freshly laundered towels heaped in the corner. She squeezed her eyes shut. The fluffy warmth of the towels, the drone of the washing machines . . . it was better than Ambien. Maybe she could sneak a nap and would finally sleep.

And then she heard the voices.

"She's dead, and we know who killed her. We have to do something . . ."

Rose's eyes snapped open.

"He killed my sister, and his brother is helping him cover it up."

She stared at the vent in the ceiling. The voice belonged to Madge Ames-Rowan.

"But what about the police? Couldn't we just talk to them? I mean, that detective seemed nice. He said he'd listen . . ." Rose could barely place the high-pitched, babyish voice of Sloane Liu. As many summers as she'd spent within an arm's reach of the girl, she couldn't remember ever hearing her speak.

"Impossible. You know who that detective is married to, right? You think they'd actually let a Club employee or her husband anywhere near him?" This voice was lower, raspy. It reeked of cigarettes at a bar all night. Lina Winthrop. It had to be.

"She's right. The police aren't an option. There's not a single person on that boat who would dare accuse one of those boys of parking in a handicapped spot, let alone murder." Madge's voice was controlled. She sounded more like a beauty queen answering her final question than a grieving stepsister.

"But how do you know . . . I mean . . . we can't be sure it was murder, right? It was probably just an accident. There's no way he'd ever intentionally . . ."

There was a scraping and shuffling above. Rose had to stand up to try to make out exactly what was being said.

". . . know exactly what they're capable of. And I know my sister. There's no way she fell off that boat, and even if she did, she won the two-hundred meter at the beginning of June. Something else happened, and whatever it was, it ended with James killing . . ."

Rose was out the door before Madge had even finished her sentence. She'd spent the last few weeks waiting for something to happen. Waiting for the chance to fix what was broken. This was it.

Madge was right. Her dad had good intentions, but there was no way in hell he'd end up charging James Gregory with murder. She was tired of the sleepless nights, of the guilt that felt like it was eating her alive from the inside out, of the disappointment in Mari's eyes. Those girls might not know it yet, but they needed her.

She slipped out of the locker room and ducked into the parlor. It was empty, but she still cast a quick look over her shoulder before throwing her weight against the massive painting of Great Grandpa Gregory's prize Great Dane, Wentworth, that lined the back wall. The wall creaked open to reveal a winding set of wooden stairs leading to the attic.

The girls had gone completely quiet above. Probably preparing to ream out the unfortunate housekeeper who had stumbled upon their little meeting . . .

But Rose wasn't a maid. And the girls didn't have the authority to kick her out. Well, not technically, anyway. Either way, she didn't care.

She'd grown up watching waitresses submit carefully worded resignations. She'd seen the way the hands of the overweight old men would casually graze her mom's body. And she could still hear her mom's matter-of-fact warning, imparted on her twelfth birthday.

"There are certain situations that I can't protect you from, Rosie. The Club has a lot to offer, but stay away from the dark rooms at the parties. If you're in the wrong place at the wrong time, no one will be able to save you. Not even me."

Chapter 6

The expression on the girls' faces said it all. Rose might as well have stormed the attic stark-naked except for a pair of cowboy boots or a sombrero or some other ridiculous "Mexican" accessory. She was doing it again.

She wasn't thinking.

And look where that had gotten her last time.

"Get. Out."

The tone of Madge's voice and the thickness of the air made Rose light-headed. She stepped backward, her memory slipping back to the beginning of July: docked, expensive yachts rocking along the pier. She'd spent an entire afternoon agonizing over the perfect outfit only to have Willa stop her in the parking lot before she'd even stepped foot on the Gregorys' ship. Quick fingers had unbuttoned her tunic, forced her out of her shorts, and tugged the scarf from her hair, cinching it around her waist instead. Madge had bitched and moaned about wasting time until Rose's shirt had become a dress, the scarf tightened around her thin waist, her wild hair unpinned and free. A tiny smile had pulled at the corner of Willa's mouth as she surveyed her handiwork. And while Madge huffed behind her sister, Rose did catch a flick of her eyebrow as she looked her up and down.

Today there was no Willa to save Rose from her stepsister. Today Rose had to fight her own battle.

"I know what you're planning, and I want to help?" Her voice was barely a whisper.

Maybe they hadn't heard her. The words had sounded so much louder in Rose's head. "Was that even English?" Lina asked.

Sloane had the decency to avert her eyes. Madge's smile was lethal, and her eyes were too bright as she advanced on Rose.

"I said I want to help." Rose practically shouted the words this time, carefully enunciating every syllable like a kid doing speech therapy exercises. As Madge drew near, Rose edged closer to the doorway.

"Fabulous." Madge stood and extended her hand, palm up. "The cost of admission is twenty-five thousand dollars."

Rose blinked.

"What? You said you wanted in, right?" Lina demanded. "Well, it's a club, and there are dues. Maybe your mom can take out a cash advance. There's got to be a Quick Cash near your house." Lina held her hand out in front of her, tilting it back and forth, assessing her nails, not bothering with eye contact.

Rose's face caught fire.

"You guys, her mom works at the Club!" Sloane cried. "We can't let her in." Rose blinked. Interesting. Maybe Sloane was the cruelest of all of them. Mocking Rose so directly, with such an obvious—

"I was *kidding*, Sloane," Lina explained.

"Now if you'll excuse us." Madge approached the attic door, positioning herself inches from Rose. She pulled the door open and raised her eyebrows, waiting for Rose to do as she'd been told.

She would never be able to look at these girls again. What had she been thinking coming up here? Did she just expect them to welcome her with open arms? Instead they made up fake dues for their ridiculous little revenge scheme. She paused to take one last look around the room, but as her foot made contact with the top step, she froze. If she left now she knew she'd never come back. And she couldn't go back to her normal life. She couldn't forget.

And then it hit her.

Before she could stop herself, she took a deep breath and spun back around. "You need me," she said with an authority that sounded completely foreign to her ears. She might as well have said the words in Spanish.

Lina sat up a little straighter, Sloane shut her mouth, and Madge lowered her arm.

"My dad is a detective. I have access to information on the Gregorys, on everyone." Rose was met with silence. She looked from the girls to the trunks and armoires and boxes of old papers and documents. The girls had as much of a history as the things in this attic, a story woven with threads of Willa. She might not have their history or their money, but if they were serious about getting revenge, she had something much more valuable.

"Whatever. Her dad's lame-ass files can't be worth twenty-five grand. Buh-bye." Lina stretched her neck over the arm of the couch.

"I might be able to help cover part of it." Sloane cocked

her head in Lina's direction. Apparently Sloane was still going with her little joke. Hilarious.

This was pretty much Rose's worst nightmare. Scorned by the very Club Brats she and Mari had spent the past three summers ripping apart. There had to be an easier way. She'd get Mari to talk to her again. She'd do whatever it took. Anything would be better than this humiliation. Rose turned to walk back down the stairs, back straight, head high. Just because she was embarking on her own personal walk of shame didn't mean she had to advertise it.

"Wait." Madge's voice stopped Rose.

She didn't turn. Madge grabbed her and spun her around.

"Welcome to the War."

"The War?" Rose repeated. She wasn't sure what side she was on.

"That's what it is, and this is what it takes if you want in." Madge paced back and forth across the room as she spoke. "You guys want to show her?" She twisted her key between her fingers while Lina and Sloane began digging through their bags.

Rose, Mari, and the rest of the staff had spent a lot of time discussing the key Madge always wore looped around her neck. Rose suspected it must open a safe where she kept her inheritance. Mari liked to imagine more sinister scenarios, her favorite being that the key unlocked a large puppy mill in the Ames-Rowan back yard.

"Twenty-five grand." Lina slapped down a stack of one hundred dollar bills. The thwack made Rose jump. "I might need some back if my dad notices the cash advance on the Amex."

Rose just stared at the pile of money. Two hundred and fifty $100 bills. $25,000 in cash. The most money she'd ever seen in her life was when her mom brought home $1,000 a member gave her as a tip after his daughter's wedding. They'd gone out to dinner to celebrate the next day. She still remembered the furrow in her dad's brow when he watched her mom pay for the meal in cash.

Sloane was still digging in her bag and finally came up with several small stacks of money and a few crumpled twenty dollar bills. "I think this is everything. If I'm short, just let me know. There might still be some money stuck in the bottom of my bag."

Rose forced herself not to stare. Lina was already sitting on the edge of the couch cushion like she expected Rose to sweep the money off the table and make a run for it.

Madge pulled something out of her pocket and made her way toward Sloane. "As discussed, the money will be kept in the bank, but if this is going to work we'll all need access." She looped a gold chain around Sloane's neck. A tiny key rested at her collarbone. "My mother left me a safety deposit box before she died. I had copies made. We're the only ones with them so our investment will be safe." She handed a necklace to Lina.

A safety deposit box. Rose had been right. Her first instinct was to text Mari. Then again, they weren't friends anymore. And they'd never be friends again, not once Mari found out about her time with these girls.

"They're engraved. *W.A.R.* Willa's initials," Madge continued matter-of-factly.

"War," Lina repeated. The girls let the word hang in the air for a moment.

"Does that make us soldiers?" Sloane asked.

"Something like that," Madge whispered. She sat up straighter. "My money is already in, and I'll make another deposit tonight." She gathered Lina's crisp bills and Sloane's wads and placed them into a large, padded envelope.

Lina and Sloane exchanged a quick glance. "Madge, we thought after everything that happened with your dad's company . . ." Lina began, but was interrupted.

"You thought wrong," Madge snapped. Sloane's cheeks turned pink. Madge's family's financial troubles weren't exactly a secret. Long before Willa died, Rose had overheard Club gossip about the Ames-Rowans' "situation." But apparently things had changed, and Madge was more than ready to contribute her share. Maybe this "War" wasn't a joke after all.

"As members of the War, you can withdraw money as you see fit. But the funds are to be used exclusively for the destruction of the Gregory family. Anything more than one thousand dollars has to be approved by all of us. Deal?"

Rose nodded along. Madge didn't have a key for her. Of course not. They couldn't have known she would show up. Nor would they trust her. But it still stung to once again be on the outside looking in. To be present, but not included.

"Have you guys ever heard of the Guardian Angels?" Madge paused directly in front of Lina and Rose, her eyes flicking between theirs.

"Aren't those the guys who fly the planes?" Sloane chirped from the chair across from them.

"Those are the Blue Angels, S," Lina said softly. Before she could stop herself, Rose let out a short bark of laughter.

"Something funny?" All five foot ten inches of Lina were up and towering over her in a split second.

Rose felt like she was walking on a tightrope. She'd assumed that Sloane was making a joke, but clearly Lina didn't think it was funny. Or maybe this was just another one of their games, another way to mess with the girl from the wrong side of the tracks.

Madge just stared at her expectantly.

"Er, I, um, it's just that . . . weren't the Guardian Angels some vigilante group from the seventies?"

"Point one for the new girl." Madge resumed her pacing and rolled her key between her fingers. "The Guardian Angels single-handedly stopped almost all of the violent crimes on subways. The police weren't doing their job," Madge looked at Rose to really drive the dig about her dad's obvious ineptitude home. "So the Guardian Angels did it for them."

"So, we're going to, like, arrest James Gregory?" The words tumbled out of Sloane's mouth. Rose felt Lina watching her and was careful to control her reaction to Sloane's comment. The whole situation was completely surreal. Sloane had the voice of a sixth grader and apparently the intellect to match. Rose didn't get it. Sloane hadn't been mean before; she'd been imbecilic. Or had she? She was a National Merit Scholar, and her parents were two of the most well-renowned doctors in the Midwest. Rose could have sworn she was dating *the* Jude Yang, who skipped three grades, had a perfect score on his ACT, and headed to Yale early. But still most surprising of all was the fact that she was actually talking. Out loud. Based on Rose's extensive observations over the past few summers, Sloane's preferred method of communication was a shake of the head, a smile, and wide eyes. Rose always thought Sloane used silence like a weapon to prove just how much smarter she was than everyone else, and she'd hated her for it. But this version of Sloane who frequently blurted out stupid thoughts was either messing with all of them or a complete idiot. Rose had no idea which.

"No arrests. And not just James. I'm suggesting we destroy

the Gregorys. All of them." Madge turned to look out the small circular window in the center of the room and opened a tin of mints, slipping one into her mouth. "James might have been the one on the boat with Willa that night, but they all had a hand in this. Covering everything up. Protecting their precious boys."

"But how do we destroy something that's indestructible with seventy-five thousand dollars and some ghetto local police files?" Lina took out her phone and started swiping and dragging her finger across the screen.

"They killed my sister." Madge's words seemed to echo in the cramped attic.

It took Rose a second to process them. Somehow Madge held both James and Trip responsible for what had happened to Willa. But that didn't make any sense. No matter how many times she tried to convince herself otherwise, everyone knew that James was with Willa when she died. How could she possibly hold Trip accountable for the sins of his brother? Trip might be a narcissistic asshole, but Rose couldn't imagine him taking anything seriously enough to be an accessory to murder. Of course, a month ago she would have said the same thing about James.

"There's no way we can take them both down. We need to focus our efforts on James. He's the one who was there." Lina didn't stop texting the entire time she talked. Her glossy nails flew across the screen as she asked all of the questions Rose wouldn't dare.

"It was both of them. You guys didn't see what I saw." Madge's voice trembled.

Rose felt the pit in her stomach grow. She might not have seen the same things Madge had seen that night, but she'd seen enough. Too much. "Trip is unstable, and James was obsessed with Willa. She got caught between them. Just because James was the last one seen with her doesn't mean Trip wasn't involved."

"James was obsessed with Willa?" Rose couldn't stop the question from slipping off the tip of her tongue.

Madge raised an eyebrow in her direction. "Uh, yeah. Where the hell have you been all summer? He totally loved her forever. He just couldn't admit it. But on the Fourth they were on in a major way. Everyone assumed they'd get married because . . ." Madge shook her head and looked back toward the window as though maybe she'd find the words she was looking for through the glass.

"But they were only seventeen!" Rose bit her lip to stop herself from saying more.

"Old money, old families, you know how it goes," Madge added.

"Actually she doesn't." Lina sniped. "Besides, their relationship was a joke. Willa loved James and James loves himself. Same old girl-loves-boy, boy-loves-his-mirror bullshit."

"Regardless," Madge interjected smoothly, "both of the Gregorys were involved, and both of them are lying about what really happened that night. Translation: they *both* need to be punished."

"This is the worst idea ever. Remember what happened to Violet Garretson when she reported James for refusing to let her get out of his car when he was wasted?" Lina paused, waiting for a response.

Rose had absolutely no idea what happened to Violet. She used to be a regular at the Club, but then she'd just sort of disappeared a couple of summers ago. There had been some rumors about rehab, but no one ever confirmed or denied anything. She was just gone.

"Well, let me jog your memory. After going to the police a couple of weeks later, someone conveniently found coke in her desk drawer. Now she gets to split her summers between Betty Ford and Jesus Camp."

Rose fully expected Madge to start sobbing on the spot. To give up. To give in. Rose felt tears welling in her own eyes, and she barely knew Willa. She looked up to prevent them from falling, but saw Sloane wipe furiously at her cheeks. Even Lina struggled to remain composed. But Madge just stood there, stone-faced.

"Girls like Violet are exactly the reason why we have to do something. I'm done letting them control me. And I refuse to sit back and let them get away with murder. What's to stop them from doing this again? There were no punishments. No repercussions." Madge fixed her eyes on Sloane. "Nothing to guarantee that this exact same thing isn't happening to your little sister two summers from now. This ends now. With us. Who's in?"

"I am," Sloane answered immediately, her eyes still shiny with tears.

"Me, too," Rose whispered, but Madge wasn't looking at her. She was staring at Lina.

"Fine. I'm in." She shook her head as if she were already regretting her decision. "But if we're going to do this, we better do it right. Nothing can ever be traced back to us. And the War is over as soon as the Gregorys are."

Madge nodded and turned to Rose. Without thinking, Rose nodded in response. Flooded with a sense of purpose, the mere act of being in this attic with these girls meant she was going to do something. Something to avenge what had happened to *their* best friend, a girl who was still a mystery to Rose. Did they know Rose was here to atone for different sins? Could they sense her secrets? Rose didn't know and she wasn't sure she cared. She was here. She was taking action. And like Mari, she was going to find her own way to rail against the Gregorys. To right their wrongs.

And then to Rose's complete surprise Madge grabbed her hand and pulled her toward the couch.

"First things first, we're going to need some information."

It was the first time Madge had ever touched Rose. Her grip felt like an anchor. They might want to destroy the Gregorys for completely different reasons, but their goal was the same. And in that moment, it bound them together like a blood oath.

Chapter 7

Rose's palms were sweaty enough to leave twin damp spots on her khaki shorts. Her knees trembled as she stood in front of the receptionist at the police station. But she kept lying.

The entire time she rambled about her dad's misplaced glasses, she thought of Trip Gregory's toothy smile. And when she slipped through the door to her dad's office, she pictured James kissing Willa. And when she typed two names into the criminal record's database, the computer dully clicking as it worked, she saw Willa's blue-tinged lips. But it was the Captain who was on her mind when she selected print and shoved the thick stack of papers into the satchel slung over her shoulder, the Captain holding forth on his yacht while Willa's body was plucked from the water.

That morning, Madge had counted out five one hundred dollar bills, explaining that Rose would probably only need a hundred, but better to be safe than sorry. It annoyed Rose to think that her "type of people" could be paid off with so little. It annoyed her even more that the three girls considered one hundred dollars to be so little. And it drove her absolutely mad that she was even considering paying off somebody in the first place. But she was in. This was War.

"Where are you off to in such a hurry?" her mom called when Rose returned home from the station.

Meat was browning on the stove top. The news blared from the television in the family room, and Rose knew without looking that her dad was camped out in his recliner either dozing or nursing a beer.

She placed a protective hand over her bag, not that anyone would ever question what was inside. She was never without whatever novel she was currently reading, and she usually toted around a few backups just in case. Her mom was always nagging her to ditch the books and actually socialize for once. If she only knew . . .

"I just want to unload some books I checked out from the library. They ordered in a few for me," Rose mumbled, half up the stairs.

"Dinner's in thirty, and I need your help with the salad!" her mom called after her, but Rose was already twisting the lock on her bedroom door, yanking the papers out from her bag. The salad could wait.

The files told a story. *The* story. They filled gaps in Rose's mind, jogged her memory of events leading up to the Fourth of July—events she couldn't completely understand until all the details were lined up in a neat row. As she skimmed the papers, the black and white picture she'd created of the Gregorys began to develop into vivid Technicolor.

Criminal background check, Charles Cornelius Gregory

III. Requesting party: Hamilton Girls and Boys Club, after-school mentor program.

Rose closed her eyes for a second and smelled rain. Her book bag had been extra heavy that day, jammed with textbooks to prepare for midterms. She'd been running, thunder pushing her forward before the skies opened up. And when they did, she didn't stop or look both ways or slow down. After the horn ripped through the driving rain, she recognized them immediately—James Gregory in the driver's seat, hands up, eyes narrowed, and Trip on the passenger side, a hand cupped over his mouth. Their ridiculous car seemed entirely out of place on the city streets, and Rose hated knowing them, or even knowing *of* them. It was all so typical. She looked like a drowned rat, while the Gregorys sat in their gleaming BMW: privileged, fortunate, dry. She had figured they either were lost or on some sort of hunt for drugs or hookers. Probably both.

But maybe she'd been wrong. At least about Trip. "Rose! Salad!" Her mom's voice yanked her from the grey downtown streets and back to her cramped bedroom.

"In a minute," she mumbled, not nearly loud enough to be heard, turning a page.

Noise complaint cited 12/31 at Gregory estate, warning issued.

Rose looked down at the pattern of flowers on her bedspread. She'd heard about the Gregorys' infamous New Year's Eve parties. The Captain rang in the New Year on some exotic island every year, but the boys stayed local. Based on the whispers that swirled around them for weeks afterward, it was the best party of the year. That is, if you could afford to go. Apparently there was a cover charge, and not to pay for some lame band or the nasty keg or even a variety of drugs lined up in some swanky bathroom like candy as Rose had always imagined. But to *play*.

Rose tapped her finger on the paper. There were at least five identical New Year's Eve citations listed in Trip's report, all resulting in a warning, a slap on the wrist, none even mentioning anything about gambling. Not that Madge, Lina, or Sloane could complain about that. Rose imagined they were there just like everyone else, blindly throwing money at whatever obstacles they might come across. The Gregorys were officially above the law. Maybe all rich people were. Maybe the rules only applied to people who didn't have thousands of dollars to spare for elaborate revenge schemes or to pay a fancy lawyer to make everything disappear.

Rose still wasn't even sure how the War girls were planning on using that much money or why it was even necessary. She couldn't help but wonder if it was more habit than anything else. Driver's license suspended? Pay off the cop. Sister killed by a drunk rich guy? Pool $75,000 and use it to destroy his family. She skimmed the remainder of Trip's file, glossing over traffic citations, fingerprint checks, one open container violation on the beach. Nothing even remotely useful . . .

She felt a little more hopeful when she opened James's file, considering his report was practically double the size of Trip's. She thought of Violet Garretson stuck in the car with him, how Madge said he wouldn't let her out. There was probably the official police report, Violet's statement. It was no secret that James was a notoriously bad drunk. He'd sobered up for a while, but he'd fallen off the wagon on July Fourth—and he was clearly off the wagon now.

Rose had to read it all. She had to know if James was the guy who had talked so passionately about moving to Montana and changing his life during their clandestine meetings—while the rest of the Club partied—or was he the spoiled rich kid who refused to take responsibility after the fact? The real James could kill the version of James she'd created in her head. Not to mention the fact that she needed $25,000 worth of information to present at the next War meeting.

The first few pages were odd. She couldn't imagine why the police would need this type of information—legal details of the Gregory family's trust fund, amended after the car accident that killed James's and Trip's parents. James Samuel Gregory was the only designated beneficiary. Rose quickly went back to Trip's file to see if she had overlooked similar paperwork about his trust fund, but it was missing. Just random language about some Cartier watches that had been in the family for years. As she continued to read, the terms of the trust were outlined, making it clear that Grandpa Gregory had included very stringent conditions as a form of incentive for James. Two stood out to Rose.

The trustee shall pay to beneficiary the terms of the trust after he earns a law degree from an accredited college or university.

The trustee shall pay to beneficiary the terms of the trust if and so long as trustee is satisfied that beneficiary conducts himself with the highest degree of honor and morality and shall not be convicted of a felony and/or a moving traffic violation.

Rose wasn't surprised that James was expected to go to college before inheriting millions. What did surprise her was the mandate that James earn a very specific degree. Apparently the Captain liked to be in the driver's seat. But what Rose found even more interesting was the second clause. Honor and morality? What a joke. As she skimmed through the few remaining pages, she came up empty. Nothing about

Violet, no DUIs, no underage drinking violations, no possession charges. Nothing. A surge of hope coursed through her body. Maybe everyone was wrong. Maybe James really wasn't the monster everyone presumed him to be. Rose let herself remember the night they met, and her surge of hope flared.

It was early June and the night was cooler than predicted. Rose wished she had grabbed her sweatshirt. Goosebumps prickled the skin along her arms and legs. Her mom had forced her into a ridiculous white dress that had barely covered her chest, and despite the fact that she was finally alone, she still pulled at the hem in an attempt to hide her cleavage.

She had been determined not to cry. She refused to think about the way her mom had ignored her or the fact that even in a room full of girls in white dresses, she was an outsider. Rose wasn't even sure why it bothered her anymore. But it did. And honestly if she was going to cry about anything, it should have been about the moment she tripped up the main stairwell, flashing her sensible underwear to the entire room below.

Surely that humiliation alone had earned her at least twenty minutes of self-indulgent hysterics.

"You know you're only supposed to cry if it's *your* party, right?" James Gregory had materialized out of nowhere.

His presence made Rose's pulse jump. She wasn't stupid. She'd heard all the rumors. Her mom's warning rang in her ears. She never should have chosen the pool house as a hideout. The tents that created the makeshift ballroom for the Club's annual Swing into Summer soiree were all the way on the other side of the grounds.

No one would hear her if she screamed.

She held her arm across her chest for coverage and avoided eye contact. James's ice clinked against the glass while he swirled the dark liquid inside, sending a tingle down her spine.

"Hey, it's okay. You're not going to get in trouble or anything." James took two long strides toward the corner Rose had wedged herself into.

"Just . . . leave me alone, okay? I know who you are and I don't want . . . I just need you to stay away from me or else I'll . . . call my dad." Rose's threat sounded beyond ridiculous even to herself. She thought of the small can of pepper spray in her brown satchel. The brown satchel that her mom had refused to let her bring to the party because it looked "low class." God, she hated her mom.

"Whoa!" James threw his hands in the air. "No need to get your dad involved. I was just looking for a place to hide for a few hours. I hate these stupid parties." He shrugged, and a smile brightened his light eyes even in the dark. It occurred to her, as they stood out in the cool night, that she'd never seen James Gregory smile. "Unless I'm wasted, apparently. Then I'm just the life of the party. Thirsty?"

"Uh, no thanks? I don't drink?"

"Is that a question or a fact? And for the record, this is just Coke."

Rose didn't know if she should believe him. He wasn't really acting like a rapist or anything. Not that she had any idea how rapists acted, but she considered herself a pretty good judge of character and despite everything she'd heard about James, she started to let her guard down. She'd even removed her arm from across her chest, though she still pined for that sweatshirt.

"Here," James said, removing his jacket and reading her

mind. "You're freezing." He'd wrapped the coat around her shoulders, and she shrugged into the warmth he left behind, breathing in the oddly appealing scent of soap and gasoline.

"Thanks," was all she had said and even then, she said it more to the ground than to him.

"You don't have to hide out here, you know. At least you didn't fall all the way *down* the stairs."

"Easy for you to say. I flashed the entire club. There's no way I'm going back in there." Her voice shook a little in the beginning, unsteady at first. She usually only talked to people at the Club who wore a nametag.

"Trust me when I say it could have been worse." One of the corners of James's mouth had lifted, and his right cheek flashed a dimple that made Rose slightly weak in the knees.

"Too bad I don't trust you at all." After she said the words it occurred to her that she was flirting with James Gregory. What the hell was she doing?

"I don't blame you. I wouldn't trust the guy who was so wasted he fell *down* the entire staircase and into his grandfather's birthday cake either."

"You didn't!"

"I did." He snorted, shaking his head. Rose couldn't help but laugh with him.

"You fell into his cake?"

"Like I said, life of the party, which is why I stick to caffeine, the safer drug." He had raised his glass, and Rose couldn't help but raise her eyebrows. It was funny how different her perception had been of James, how quickly it could change, even during one short conversation. He actually wasn't so bad.

"Guess that's the point of rehab," he mumbled.

His confession made Rose feel better somehow. She didn't need any reminder how imperfect she was; it was just nice to know that other people felt the same way about themselves.

A loud knock at her bedroom door shook her from the beginning of the summer, a few papers fluttering off the bed as she startled. "Rose! I've called you three times. Dinner's ready, no thanks to you." Her mom stomped back down the stairs as Rose gathered the papers, skimming James's section one last time before shoving the pile beneath her pillow.

There was absolutely no reference to a stint in rehab, no drug or alcohol-related infractions anywhere in his file. He had no reason to lie about his history, especially to her.

Either her dad was worse with paperwork than she thought or the Gregorys really were above the law.

Chapter 8

Rose liked to play a game during family dinners where she challenged herself to speak fewer than ten words the entire meal. It started out as a power thing. Some girls took to starvation when they wanted to bug the shit out of their mothers, but Rose liked food too much. Besides, there was nothing that upset Pilar McCaan more than awkward silence. The average dinner conversation word count fell somewhere between nine and twenty, but one time last winter she successfully made it through an entire meal mumbling only three words. (Granted, her parents were fighting about putting a new roof on the house the entire time, but Rose still considered it an accomplishment.)

"I happened to overhear that you and James Gregory had quite the run in at the Club today," her mom commented, piling Rose's plate with lasagna.

Rose took a huge bite. The good old chew-and-shrug, a classic maneuver . . .

"What have I told you about the Gregorys? They're trouble."

Rose felt like replying with, "You're a hypocrite," but didn't want to waste three words. Besides, her mouth was full.

"Your mother is right. Be careful with the Gregorys."

To this day, Rose could never tell if her dad simply parroted whatever her mom said or if he knew more than he let on. Neither garnered much respect. Her phone vibrated in her pocket. She managed to slide it onto her lap while barely moving, another one of her many talents.

War meeting in 20. Same place.

She quickly choked down the rest of her lasagna and cleared her plate.

"What's the rush, Rosie?" She hated her dad's nickname for her. The only people named Rosie were chubby three-year-olds and overweight comedians.

"Meeting some friends." Three words. She was still in this.

"What friends? Where are you going? Pilar, did you know about this?" Her dad looked at her mom, but she was busy on her own phone, her full lips turned up in a half smile. Rose knew that smile, and she couldn't unknow it. No matter how many times she tried. That smile gave Rose a pit in her stomach, like she'd barged in on her mom in the shower, singing for no reason Rose or her dad could imagine.

"What?" Her mom's cheeks flushed. "I mean, of course. Whatever. Just don't be late, okay Rose?"

"Okay." Four words total. Almost her record. Her dad waved her out the door, his dark eyes fixed on her mom as she sat at the table hunched over her phone.

Rose had a feeling there was another argument brewing, something more complicated than a new roof. But she couldn't worry about that now. She grabbed a sweatshirt and stuffed the Gregorys' files back in her satchel before heading out the front door. If she walked fast she could get there in ten minutes.

The sun was making its final descent along the horizon, the surrounding sky grey and pink in its wake. A breeze shifted leaves on the trees hugging the sidewalk, and Rose quickened her steps, wondering if it would rain. She finally felt like she could breathe again without the heat wrapping its sticky fingers around her neck. Maybe she'd even start sleeping like a normal person again.

The smell of freshly cut grass and lush magnolias made her sneeze exactly ten times, her cue that she was getting close to the Club. Rose was a serial sneezer, and nothing brought it on quite like Hawthorne Lake's carefully manicured lawns.

After she pulled open the Club's impressive double doors, she kept her eyes trained on the floor and raced in the direction of the parlor. She'd need the room to be empty so she could access the hidden entrance. Of course, she heard a muffled voice trailing out from behind the door. A man she'd never seen before stood in front of the floor-to-ceiling window, a phone gripped to his ear, his voice clipped and strained. He glanced at her irritably. After a few awkward moments, he rolled his eyes at her and left in a huff. When she finally scrambled up to the attic, she was sweating like a tourist, all pit stains and pleated shorts. Honestly, she didn't even blame the girls for the disgust on their faces. Plus, she was late and they'd been busy. The attic was lit with at least thirty candles and they had old yearbooks and newspapers scattered all over the floor.

"Nice of you to join us." Madge nodded toward the empty seat next to her. "The yearbooks and newspapers are courtesy of some sorry excuse for a first-year who was entirely too easy to pay off. So far we've learned that Trip was voted Class Clown, huge shocker there, while James was elected Darcy-In-Training. I suppose his air of asshole made him quite the object of affection at Pemberly Brown."

Rose sat in the chair across from her.

"Right, so our current plan is to destroy them using a hilarious, modern-day Elizabeth Bennet," Lina added. "Surely their heads will explode." She rolled her eyes and examined an old issue of a school newspaper.

"Um, didn't Willa kind of already do that?" Sloane's tone was innocent. Clearly she didn't mean to be an insensitive moron, but the fire in Madge's eyes was enough to force Rose into tipping her hand.

"I've got something," she offered. The girls turned to her. What if they thought her idea was ridiculous? Or what if she'd misread the papers in the file? This was going to end in disaster, she just knew it. And who the hell had decided that candles were a good idea for an attic at the end of July?

"Spit it out, Rose," Lina grumbled. "You're not paying dues like the rest of us, so you better have something good."

Rose swallowed and forced herself to speak. "Their trust fund has this weird morality clause where they lose their inheritance if they don't conduct themselves to the Captain's standards. If they're convicted of a felony or even if they so much as get a speeding ticket, they're totally cut off."

"You've got to be shitting me." Lina's eyes narrowed. She glanced at Madge. Sloane started shaking her head.

"No, really, it's all right here." Rose placed the papers in the center of the circle.

All three girls crawled forward, their heads nearly touching in the flickering candlelight. Rose held her breath. The seconds ticked by with agonizing slowness.

"She's right," Madge whispered, sitting back on her heels. "It actually kind of makes sense now. That's why everyone turns the other way. If they mess up they lose everything." She smiled, a glint in her eyes. "This could work."

"Well, I don't know," Rose said. She chewed her lip. "It might be kind of hard to get them disinherited. This is a whole new level." The image of James weeks ago at the pool house flashed in her mind. He didn't seem like a murderer then. As if they sensed her inner turmoil, the girls all began talking at once.

"This will be nothing compared to what he did to Willa," Sloane chirped.

Lina nodded sagely. "To a Gregory, the only thing worse than being dead is being poor."

"You're a genius, Rose." Madge grabbed Rose's hand, pressing something small and hard into her palm. When she pulled away and opened her fingers, she saw a long gold chain with a tiny key attached. Her heart began to pound.

"What the hell, Madge?" Lina barked. "We talked about this. You can't give her that key. We don't know anything about her."

Rose should have been used to being talked about like she wasn't in the room, but she wasn't. Maybe that was one of those things you never got used to.

"She's proven herself." Madge narrowed her eyes at Lina. "I trust her."

Rose's head was spinning. She had proved herself worthy of the War. She might not have money, but she had information, and Rose was beginning to believe that real power came with knowledge, not a checking account.

Rose had never been on a boat so big that you didn't even notice the gentle rocking of the water. The deck floor gleamed in the clear moonlight, waxed and shiny. A low mumble of voices mixed with the thump of distant music poured from every direction. Clusters of people hung along the perimeter, chatting, sipping, laughing. If they noticed her, she probably would have just turned around and left. She was sure if anyone actually looked at her they would have laughed at her outfit or feigned sympathy for the lost expression permanently creasing her brow.

But as usual, Rose was invisible, and tonight, she was glad for it.

Tonight invisibility gave her a chance to figure out which direction to go. Up, down, around? The yacht was so large that the options seemed endless. In truth, she was terrified. She'd lied to her parents about going to some lame church festival with school acquaintances because she knew they'd never let her within twenty thousand feet of the S.S. Gregory. Yes, the Gregorys actually named their yacht after themselves without even the slightest hint of irony. Well, all of them except James anyway.

Wasn't that what brought her here? The thrill of James, and the time they'd spent together in secret? The way they'd laughed about how ridiculous his self-involved family really was? The look on his face when Rose told him about her parents' fights? The way his lips grazed hers lightly whenever he said goodbye, a whisper against hers, like a promise he intended to keep? James had begged her to come. His family's annual Fourth of July bash was his own personal hell. Last year he'd fallen off the wagon. It was almost impossible to avoid the temptations aboard the ship. But if he had some-one to escape with, someone like Rose, then maybe this year would be different.

Rose yanked her dress down to cover her butt as she climbed the stairs to the main deck. She was deeply apprecia-tive of Willa's impromptu makeover, but she was also 99% sure that it was going to result in another massive, ass-baring wardrobe malfunction.

Maybe the generous expanse of leg on display tonight would finally be enough to tempt James into doing more than just kissing her. They'd snuck off into hidden corners of the Club every chance they had since the night of the Swing. But he never tried anything besides kissing, and Rose was too shy to let her hands roam anywhere south of his chest. Tonight was the night. It had to be. Rose shook her head. Even think-ing about being with James made it feel too much like a jinx.

She stretched her neck to the right, evaluating the clusters of people in the moonlight. The music she'd heard when she walked aboard had all but disappeared, replaced by the drone of conversation. Diamonds sparkled on necks and ears and fingers. She watched as an older woman laughed, raking her manicured nails down the arm of a man who eyed her hungrily despite being nearly surgically attached to the woman on his other arm. The adult section of the party: exactly where she didn't want to be. If anyone from the Club recognized her, it would get back to her mom, and she couldn't imagine what might happen after that. She turned the other way. The stairwell to the bottom deck of the ship was blocked by velvet rope. A bouncer in a tux held a basket of cell phones in one hand, embossed cards in the other. He bowed as Rose approached. "Welcome aboard, Miss. Please take a phone."

"Um, I already have my phone, so I'm all set." Rose tried to push past him, but the bouncer deftly blocked her entrance.

"Every lady must accept a phone."

Rose looked behind her, confused. One of the boys she recognized from the pool approached and grabbed a card from the basket. He nodded at the bouncer and gave Rose's all-too-accessible butt a little squeeze.

"Wouldn't mind dialing your digits tonight." He winked and disappeared into the crowd of people dancing and mingling inside.

"What the . . ."

Just then, Willa Ames-Rowan scooted around Rose and grabbed a phone. "It's like spin the bottle," she whispered. "Guys text girls to meet up in one of the fancy rooms."

Rose blinked. She began to feel sick.

Willa touched Rose's arm, grazing her skin just as lightly as James's lips had grazed her mouth. Her expression was serious. "Don't do anything that makes you uncomfortable, okay? If it rings and you're not into it, just hit ignore. Easy."

She grabbed a phone out of the basket and turned around to look at Rose again. "Oh, and stay away from James. He's spoken for tonight." Willa waved her phone in front of Rose's face, her smile so disarming that it took Rose a minute to understand what she was saying.

"Um, yeah. Okay?" Rose tried to avoid Willa's eyes, questions flooding her brain but never making it past her lips. She knew Willa liked James. Everyone knew Willa liked James. But now that Rose had spent so much time with James she thought it was just gossip. Rumors. Truthfully, she hadn't really thought about it at all.

Willa pressed a phone into Rose's hand. "Everything is going to be fine. No, better than fine, it's going to be fabulous," and she smiled her heartbreaking smile again.

Rose looked at her closely, trying to see past the perfect teeth and the sparkling blue eyes, searching for a hint of anger, resentment, or even laughter. Maybe this was all some big joke. But that smile was genuine. If Willa did know about the time Rose was spending with James, she didn't hate her for it. Or maybe she just didn't see Rose as competition. Maybe James had been in love with Willa all along, and Rose was just some pathetic Club employee's daughter he'd been stringing along for fun.

The phone felt like a time bomb ticking in Rose's hand. Taking it felt like making a promise she had no intention of keeping, but Rose couldn't force herself to let it go. She wanted to make a run for it. To throw the phone back at the weird guy standing there in the tux. Willa walked into the party to join her friends, and Rose looked back toward the upper deck, searching for a way out. The adults looked like they were beginning to feel the effects of all that top-shelf gin. Rose stiffened as she saw the Captain grab a petite woman with long black hair toward a shadowy corner at the top of the stairs. His third wife was a statuesque blonde. Something about the way the other woman moved reminded Rose of her . . .

Mom.

Rose recognized Pilar the second the Captain tipped her face up toward the moonlight. His lips were on hers almost immediately. Rose's stomach twisted. She couldn't move, but she couldn't look away. The Captain's hands moved under her mom's dress. She stared so long and so hard that some long defunct mother-daughter bond must have been activated, because all at once her mom froze and looked down to exactly where Rose was standing.

She tried to duck into the shadows, but the look on her mom's face told her it was too late. So, in the end, the choice was made for her. Rose squeezed the phone and walked into the party. The tears pricking her eyes only made her more determined to find James. She'd find him and ask him why the hell he'd invited her to a party when there were girls like Willa Ames-Rowan falling all over him. She pushed through the crush of teenagers dancing, drinking and laughing. Her eyes scoured the crowd for his shaggy blond hair, those dark blue eyes . . . for the one person who might actually be able to redeem this horrible night.

And then she saw him.

With Willa.

She was on her tiptoes, her lips on his ear. James swayed uneasily on his feet, brown liquor sloshing dangerously in his glass. And then he wrapped his arms around her, wove his fingers through her perfect blonde hair, his mouth crashing down on hers.

Rose wanted to be off that boat more than she'd ever wanted anything in her entire life. She looked out one of the circular windows, to the water sloshing over the glass. And she debated. If the phone in her hand hadn't vibrated, she would have climbed back up, jumped into the dark water, and swam back to shore.

Harbinger's Port in 10.

But instead Rose took a different leap. She grabbed an abandoned bottle of champagne on her way past the bar and took a long swallow. Staggering through an endless maze of narrow hallways, she ignored the noises that floated out from underneath the doors. Instead she focused on each room's pretentious-sounding name. Mariner's Cove, Caleb's Corner, Lawrence Bay . . . By the time she came to the door with a shiny plaque engraved with Harbinger's Port, she had finished off the bottle of champagne. Warmth slowly spread from her stomach out to her fingers and toes. It made her smile, made everything feel right. She abandoned the bottle beside the door and turned the handle.

Rose slipped across the threshold, pressing her backside against the door to click it shut. She needed the darkness if she was going to go through with any of this. It snuffed out everything—inhibitions, fear, reality. Her eyes worked frantically to adjust before she moved forward. But she heard him breathing before she could even make out the outline of his body.

He laughed quietly as she approached.

"I was hoping it'd be you."

He kissed her roughly on the mouth, and she kissed him back even harder. He pressed her down into the bed, and she raised her body to meet him, to feel him.

She told herself it didn't matter who it really was.

She told herself she was ready even as Willa's voice ran on repeat in her mind. "Don't do anything that makes you uncomfortable. Don't do anything that makes you uncomfortable. Don't do anything . . ."

She didn't look back. Not even when the light from the large window overlooking the lake caught on his red hair and she recognized Trip Gregory. He was probably pretending she was someone else, but Rose didn't care because she was pretending he was James.

When it was over she couldn't look at him, she just lay on her side, her eyes wide open drinking in the blackness of the room. Even after she heard him get dressed and quietly shut the door, she couldn't force herself to follow. Instead she stared at the ceiling thinking about James and Willa and all that she'd lost that night. She lay there for what felt like hours. She lay there until she heard the sound of the fireworks exploding in the night sky and only then did she force herself to pull her body from the bed. Too humiliated to turn on the lamp, she dressed slowly, finding her clothes as occasional bursts of light illuminated the way. Ironic: everyone else on this boat was celebrating. They knew nothing of Rose's humiliation or how much she had given up to be on the boat that night. They had all turned a blind eye. While some danced, others drowned.

PART 2

C.O.I.N. (Counterinsurgency)

Chapter 9

It took all of Lina's flinty determination to remain focused on painting her fingernails a deep inky blue. Madge was practically dancing around the attic, spouting off ideas to destroy the Gregorys. Lina wasn't sure what it was about Rose McCaan, but she couldn't quite trust her. Everyone had an agenda, an angle. So what was Rose's? She wasn't friends with Willa. Not the way the rest of them were. Her mother was a Club employee working for the Captain, and her dad was the detective who had let James Gregory walk free. There was no way she would be willing to risk her parents for some girl she barely even knew. There was something she wasn't telling them. Something she was hiding. Lina was sure of it.

"It's perfect. We'll plan something epic, and they'll lose everything. No more country club, no more inheritance. Nothing." Madge's face glowed in the flickering light of the candles. "And after they've lost it all, maybe then the truth will come out. Maybe they'll finally pay."

"But how . . ." The words were barely past Rose's lips before Sloane tactlessly interrupted.

"So . . . we're going to steal all their money?"

Lina's fingers tensed around the bottle of nail polish. Her eyes snapped to Rose, daring her to react. *Just try it.* Lina had put a lot of time and effort into training herself to ignore the things in her life that she couldn't control, so she didn't really see much point in this War. After years of doing everything she could to get her parents' attention (including but not limited to: chopping off all of her ridiculously long black hair and dying it white-blonde, getting tattoos that snaked up and down her arms, and carefully creating a reputation for being a total slut), she had come to terms with their complete ambivalence about their only daughter's well-being. She learned to forget that she even had parents.

When they'd pulled Willa's body out of the lake, Lina knew just as well as everyone else on that yacht that James Gregory had killed one of her best friends. What she also knew was that talking to the police would result in her exile from the Club. And the Club was all Lina had. So she ignored that, too. And, of course, her lips were sealed for reasons she'd never be able to admit to herself—let alone anyone else.

She understood why Madge wanted revenge. She wanted to punish the Gregorys just as much. But Lina made it a point never to fight losing battles, and there was no doubt in her mind that they were going to fail miserably. She'd handed Madge her money and she'd be there for her friends. There was no way she was going to bail after what happened to Willa, but that didn't mean she had to put up with bullshit from this new girl. To make matters worse, Rose clearly didn't know what to make of Sloane.

When they were ten, Lina was the only girl not invited to

Carlisle McCord's birthday party. Sloane faked a stomach-ache, and they'd lounged around Sloane's house slurping homemade chicken noodle soup at Mrs. Liu's insistence. When Lina's parents failed to show before winter holiday at Rennert, her boarding school, the headmistress made arrangements for her to board over break—that is, until Sloane drove all the way up to collect her. It was the best Christmas she could remember, filled with more pie than anyone needed, roaring fires, and presents with *Lina* hand-written on tags as though she'd been part of the Liu family since birth. Sloane guarded Lina silently. Her rescues were never discussed. They just happened. Protect and be protected. So, yeah, she'd be damned if she was going to let some trashy event planner's daughter mock Sloane. But as Lina opened her mouth to answer Sloane's ridiculous question, Madge beat her to it.

"No one's stealing anything." Even in her frenzied state Madge was careful to be patient with Sloane. "We're just going to show the Captain that his grandsons are a couple of assholes undeserving of his precious inheritance. And hopefully reveal the fact that James is a cold-blooded murderer at the same time."

"Easier said than done," Lina mumbled under her breath.

Madge must not have heard her. Or she was just ignoring her. Either way she dragged Rose over to a pair of chairs situated near the wall and began whispering plans.

Lina felt a quick stab of jealousy. She had always been the person Madge planned with. The idea girl. But ever since everything with Willa, things had changed. Madge was distant. Distracted. Lina tried not to be hurt. The girl's stepsister had just died, after all. Madge had every right to retreat within herself, to mourn and hide in private. But as Lina watched Madge and Rose beneath her lowered lashes, she wondered if perhaps she was being replaced. There was something about the way Rose kept touching the key around her neck that made Lina want to scream. Why couldn't anyone else see that this girl couldn't be trusted?

"Lina, Lina, ballerina why so quiet?" Sloane plopped down on the couch and knocked the bottle of blue polish over, splattering it across Lina's legs and the hem of her shift dress.

"Jesus!" The word was out of Lina's mouth before she could bite it back. She shot up from the couch and started dabbing at the blue streaks of paint with a discarded beach towel. Lina couldn't have given two shits about the dress. She had dozens more just like it in her closet, but the muddy blue mess at the end of her fingertips burst a delicate bubble of rage inside her. Her nails were always perfect. Well, they were since Willa died, anyway. Lina remembered when she and Willa stayed up all night trying to create the perfect ombre manicure. Willa had found some article online with step-by-step instructions. But they'd kept bumping their nails against the coffee table or accidentally smudging them when reaching into the big white bowl that sat between them for a handful of popcorn. Madge had made fun of them for walking around with salt smudged nails the next day, but they laughed and said it only added to the effect. If Willa were there she would have already convinced Lina that the nail polish splattered across her dress and over the tips of her fingers was a fashion statement.

But Willa was dead.

Tears sprang to Lina's eyes.

"I'm sorry . . . I just . . . I need some air." She backed out of the room and rushed down the stairway, hurtling into the parlor, not caring if anyone saw—then out the French doors to one of the Club's massive patios. She bent over as though she'd be sick.

"Hey, are you okay?"

The voice came from a shadowed stoop in front of one of the side doors. Lina squinted through the darkness but could only make out the red tip of a cigarette and a long pair of legs, crossed at the ankles. But then the girl leaned forward, catching the light, and Lina recognized her wavy hair immediately. *Mari.* The waitress who was supposedly involved with Trip Gregory. Lina hadn't seen her around the Club since the Fourth. She had heard she'd been fired . . . which was fine by her.

"I'm fine," Lina said. "Leave me alone." She turned to go back inside. It wasn't the first time this girl had stumbled upon Lina, and there was no way she was up for a repeat performance of what had happened on the Gregorys' yacht. Not tonight.

"Wait." Mari exhaled a cloud of smoke and dropped the butt to the ground, grinding out the ash with her sandal. "We need to talk. About that night . . ."

Lina whirled around. "I have nothing to say to you. Go find Trip. Talk to him. You guys seem to have plenty to discuss." Her stony mask was firmly back in place and she noted with satisfaction how each word cut into her target like tiny darts. Mari wasn't worth her time.

Lina pressed her shoulders back as far as she could and turned back toward the entrance of the Club, forcing the bones of her back to jut out like wings as she walked. She was Lina Winthrop. She was tough. She was strong. She took what she wanted and didn't give a shit about what anyone said or thought.

"You know where to find me when you're ready to talk," the girl called after her.

Despite herself, Lina turned one more time. But there was

no evidence of Mari, save for the cigarette butt that still smol-
dered on the concrete.

Find me. The words echoed in her head.

Suddenly she had the perfect idea for their first battle. For
the first time that night a small smile played across Lina's
face, and when she climbed the stairs back up to the attic,
she felt a surge of adrenaline snake its way through her veins.
Lina Winthrop was back in the driver's seat. It would only
be a matter of time before she was looking at the crumpled
forms of James and Trip Gregory in her rearview mirror.

Chapter 10

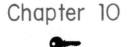

Lina took the stairs two at a time and burst into the attic. "I have an idea," she said, curling her fingers beneath the hem of her stained dress. She tried to catch Sloane's eye, to offer a silent apology, but Sloane deliberately avoided her gaze. Lina knew she deserved it.

"Trip is sleeping with some whore of a waitress. We use her as bait." Lina thought of Mari with her full lips and mocha skin. She was a sure thing.

Madge's eyebrow flicked subtly and Lina knew she'd struck a chord. So she took the opportunity to shift into third and flood the gas. She strode toward one of the chairs in the middle of the room and sat down without saying another word.

"Um, which girl are you talking about exactly?" Rose asked. The words seemed to catch in her throat. She grabbed her bottled water and started chugging.

"Mari." Lina scowled and continued. "Anyway, Trip dialed my number on the yacht. He might not be the hot brother. Not to mention, everyone knows he's completely unstable after he pretty much killed his own parents . . . but he knows what he's doing." She smiled wickedly for effect. She was pleased to see Rose's mouth fall open, and her cheeks burst into flame. If there was one thing Lina had perfected it was the art of shock value. She only hoped she'd shock them enough to hide the fact that her being with Trip was a lie. "That waitress walked in and caused the biggest scene. Apparently she actually thought they were dating. Like a Gregory would ever date *staff.*" As soon as Lina uttered the word staff, Rose gasped and began choking. Lina seized the opportunity to see how her little story was going over with Madge and Sloane. Their wide-eyed stupor said it all. She had them exactly where she wanted them. She stared pointedly at Rose, waiting for her to stop hacking away.

"S-s-sorry. Wrong tube," Rose finally managed.

"You don't have to be here, you know. You're free to leave at any time."

Madge lifted her hand in the air to stop Lina from going any further. They'd already had this conversation and clearly Madge wasn't in the mood to have it again. Lina rolled her eyes and continued. "As I was saying, we blackmail her. Force her to confess. Trip goes down and . . ."

"I don't see how blackmailing some poor girl will get us anywhere," Madge said. "And what about James? This isn't good enough."

"Pictures," Rose whispered. Her voice was still hoarse.

Lina's dark eyes sliced through Rose's.

"No one can deny pictures." Rose lowered her eyes as she said it. "What if we took compromising pictures? Trip with the waitress. James with . . . someone else. We show them to everyone. The Captain is forced to disinherit. We win."

Lina didn't like Rose's use of the word "we." In fact, Lina didn't like any of this. Not Rose. Not Rose's taking her idea and making it better. Not being forced out. She picked at the nail polish that had dried around the edges of her ring fingernail until she saw blood.

"The only thing James has been hitting lately is a bottle of whiskey," Lina knew she was contradicting her own plan but she couldn't stop herself.

Rose fidgeted. Her foot shook up and down, and Lina was reminded of courtroom dramas when convicted criminals were put on the stand. What was her deal? Lina considered calling her out, putting her on the spot again, but she knew it would only annoy Madge. But what exactly was Rose hiding? What did she know? Sometimes the way Rose looked at Lina made her wonder if she'd seen Lina on that boat. If she knew what she'd done. The thought of someone else—a stranger—knowing her secret made her skin crawl.

"I can get James?"

At first Lina wasn't sure she'd heard her right, what Rose had just done did not even qualify as speaking. More like opening her mouth and releasing air.

"Speak up. I don't even think *you* heard you." Lina said even though she knew exactly what Rose had muttered. It was the words that really pissed her off, not the volume.

"I can get James." Rose said each word slowly, lifting her eyes at the end, punctuating her statement.

"How?" Madge asked. Sloane held a page of the yearbook in midair waiting patiently for Rose's response. Lina stood by the door, hating herself for waiting, too.

"He texts me. We're friends. I mean . . . we *were* friends."

That was it. Lina pounced.

"So, what you're saying is that you're friends with the guy

who killed our best friend. Is that right?" She raked her blue fingers through her hair and shook her head. "You just show up in here claiming to want to help take down a family you know nothing about! To get revenge for a girl who didn't even know you *existed*." Lina turned toward Madge and Sloane. "Am I the only one who wants to know what she's *really* doing here?"

"Lina!" Sloane shouted, slamming the yearbook shut. "We all know you miss her. We all do. But you don't have to be such a bitch."

Lina had never heard Sloane curse, let alone at her. And the worst part was that Sloane was right. Lina couldn't even think of anything clever to say. She'd failed in every way possible.

"Enough." Madge stood. Her eyes flickered orange in the candlelight, tiger-like. "None of this is going to work if we can't get along. I'm not asking anyone to be friends. Willa held us together. But she's gone, and this only works if we're a team."

Madge was right. None of this would ever have happened if Willa were alive. Lina brushed her fingers over her first tattoo, a huge snake that wound its way up her left arm. Madge had been horrified when she'd seen it for the first time, had dubbed Lina "white trash." Sloane had stared at her like she had no idea who she was. But Willa had walked right over to her and ran her fingers over the ink.

"*Does it hurt?*" she'd asked. Looking back, Lina wondered if she'd been asking about the tattoo at all. Willa hadn't waited for an answer; instead she squeezed Lina's hand lightly and announced that if Lina was officially white trash they might as well celebrate with Cheetos and beef jerky. Everyone had laughed, and Madge apologized over a Slim Jim for being such a bitch, and everything had righted itself.

But tonight there was no Willa to diffuse the tension. Tonight there would be no impromptu gas station run. Tonight there was only Lina and her regrets.

"You're right, Sloane," Lina murmured. "I miss her." She stopped short of apologizing to Rose. She wasn't sorry for questioning the girl, and she still couldn't imagine how her friends were able to trust a virtual stranger. Maybe trust was less complicated when you didn't have anything to hide. "I'll try harder," she added. The words sounded gravelly as she pushed them past the burning in her throat.

Madge clapped her hands together. "Excellent. Lina, you take the waitress and Trip. Rose, you do whatever it takes with James. Get pictures. The dirtier the better. We'll project them the night of the gala. Don't let me down."

Meeting adjourned.

Chapter 11

Lina lingered around the outskirts of the Club the next day, hoping to fly under the radar. She wore her favorite pair of oversized sunglasses in a pathetic attempt to disguise herself. If anything, the huge shades made her closely cropped, white-blonde hair stand out that much more. At least the rest of her outfit was ordinary, boring, and practical. She wore the only pair of shorts she owned and an army green ribbed tank top. But she drew the line at her lips and nails. In Lina's experience, it was impossible not to be in control when wearing Big Apple Red nail polish and Venetian Red lipstick.

Dew-drenched grass tickled Lina's toes as she wove her way along the path through the woods—laser-focused on making it to the Club's basketball courts before Trip Gregory's weekly game began.

When she found a large tree with a perfect hidden view, she surveyed the branches, tucked her phone into her bra band and began climbing. Her bright red nails looked shiny and out of place against the peeling bark of the tree, her muscles taut as she climbed. Only when Lina settled into the gentle curve of a thick branch did she let the tension ease slowly from between her clenched shoulders. The court was still empty, the green asphalt pristine.

She was here. She was ready. She was in control.

Lina fished out her phone and scrolled through the texts. Rose was driving her crazy with her plan for James Gregory. Apparently she'd figured out a way to get him out of his pants, but she needed Lina to play photographer. She still couldn't get past the fact that Rose and James were a thing. There was no doubt in Lina's mind that their relationship somehow played into Rose's real agenda for joining the War. Her only hope was that seeing Rose and James interact tonight would finally give Lina the proof she needed to get rid of Rose McCaan for good. An image of Willa wrapping a scarf around Rose's waist the night of the party surfaced in Lina's mind, unbidden. Willa had been prone to picking up strays. Jessa Phillips the summer of third grade, Nora Williams in fifth, but it wasn't until the summer of seventh that she'd found Carolina Winthrop.

Metal clanked as the door to the courts swung open and then shut again.

"Game on," she whispered under her breath. She clicked on her camera phone.

The first boy through the gate wasn't Trip. It was actually someone Lina didn't recognize as a club member. A busboy. Rory Something. He walked the length of the court, right beneath Lina. Her pulse quickened. She held her breath. She hoped if she remained frozen, he wouldn't be prickled by that feeling of another presence, the feeling of being watched. All he'd have to do is look up and she'd be screwed. Rory threw a duffle bag down against the fence, swearing when something spilled out. Small white pills rolled every which way. He jumped to stop them, furtively scooping the stash back into the container just as more players arrived. *Interesting.* Clearly busboy liked his meds, and liked them secret.

Trip entered the court wearing his trademark cocky smile. Other boys followed, doing the handshake-shoulder-bump that every phys ed teacher must teach males when they separate the sexes and roll condoms onto bananas. Her jaw tightened. It was as if nothing had changed. Of course, for them, nothing really had.

As they started to play, she spotted James Gregory waltzing slowly toward the gate. His eyes were hidden behind aviator sunglasses, and he sat on the bench near the courts. She stared at him looking bored out of his skull while the game around him continued, sweaty and violent. Trip threw elbows, talked trash, and generally kicked ass. She couldn't help but be impressed. No wonder he'd wanted the basketball court relocated closer to the main grounds. After maybe ten minutes, the boys took a water break. Rory spent the majority of his time chatting up a very unengaged looking James until Trip joined the party, slapping both of the boys on the back. She couldn't catch the exact words; she was breathing too heavily and her phone shook in her hands, but a laugh exploded from Trip's chest. The sound rolling over the court and spilling into the woods beyond.

Without warning, he threw the ball across the court in one of those "look at me, I need attention every second of the day" kind of shots. It clanged the rim and bounced toward the fence. Trip jogged to retrieve the ball, but kicked it instead—which was odd. It rolled directly in front of Rory's duffle. Lina held her breath again, watching Trip scoop up the ball while discreetly plucking the bottle of pills from the open zipper and tucking them into the pocket of his mesh shorts. *Guess that rules out allergy medicine*, Lina thought. She raised her phone to her eyes. If only she had super-zoom so she could actually see what drugs he'd just stolen.

Water bottles were emptied; players swiped the backs of their hands across their mouths and used their shirts to wipe the sweat from their faces. In the meantime, Trip trotted back to James who dug money from his bag to hand to Rory. *Unbelievable*. The scene below came into crisp focus. Trip hadn't stolen a thing. She'd just witnessed the most discreet drug deal in the history of mankind.

The bark from the branch dug into Lina's bony butt and she prayed the boys would finish soon. She was sweating. All at once, her fingers slipped and she lost her grip on the phone. It made a dull thump when it landed, partially concealed by a low shrub. A few boys turned to the sound, stretching their necks to survey the woods, but gave up and turned back to their game. Not Trip. His eyes were narrowed in the direction of Lina's tree. He jogged to the edge of the fence, cocking his head, not a dozen feet below her. Lina made her lanky body as small as possible along the tree branch. Waiting.

Willa. Willa. Willa.

Lina couldn't understand why she mentally repeated Willa's name, but it was as though every thought had been washed away. Her friend's name was the only word that remained—a mantra. Was she praying? She didn't know; she just needed Trip to walk away.

And then he did.

She would have thought in that moment that Willa would feel closer, more alive, eternal almost. After all, she'd answered Lina's prayers. Or someone had. But instead, it was just a stark reminder that Willa was dead. Gone. Ashes scattered. All because of a boy who hung around a country club, bought drugs, and lived his life like nothing had changed. In that moment she wanted to jump down from the tree and destroy every stupid boy on that court. On some level they were all in this together. It was the way Hawthorne Lake worked, with its secrets and cover-ups and dismissive "boys will be boys" rules. And it would happen again. To another girl. Another friend. Another sister.

For a moment Lina swayed on the branch thinking about how good it would feel to rake her red nails across James's inscrutable face. But instead, she stilled herself, tilting her face to the sky, allowing the light filtering through the leaves above to paint her body with splashes of sun. Lina waited. She felt something inside her stir; something that felt dangerously close to hope, and for the first time since she'd handed Madge $25,000, she thought they might actually be able to do this. She finally had physical, undeniable proof of the Gregory boys breaking the law. Proof that might finally force the Captain to disinherit them both. Maybe power wasn't an illusion after all. Maybe it was out there for the taking just as long as you knew where to find it. Or at least how to fight for it.

Chapter 12

After what felt like an eternity, the boys disbanded and headed back to the main Club grounds. Lina shimmied down the tree, reaching up to the sky and bending to touch her toes at the bottom. She felt as if she'd just emerged from the trunk of someone's car. She bent to retrieve her phone: all in one piece and still operational. She sent a silent *thank you* up to Willa.

But before weaving back through the woods, Lina slipped onto the basketball court and got down on her hands and knees, surveying the ground near where Rory's duffle had been. Two cigarette butts, a candy wrapper, grass clippings . . . and *yes*. A lone white pill had slipped into one of the cracks near the edge of the court. Using her nail to pop it out, she examined the stamped name. Xyrem. She frowned, pulling up Google on her phone. Now she was even more confused. What the hell did Trip want with a drug used to treat narcolepsy? She clicked on the Wikipedia link, her eyes flashing down to three letters she recognized instantly.

XYREM is a kind of GHB. XYREM can cause very low

levels of awareness (or consciousness), with some cases of coma and death.

Trip and James had just purchased a date rape drug. A drug that James could have given to Willa the night she died. A drug that would explain why one of the best swimmers at the Club drowned in the lake on a night when the water was as still as glass. The words on the screen in front of her blurred and swam together. She snapped a photo of the pill, tucked it in her pocket and ran the entire length of the trail back to the sunroom.

"What can I do for you, Ms. Winthrop?" The girl behind the bar looked bored, and Lina was overwhelmed by the smell of sickeningly sweet vanilla lotion. Lina wanted to tell her that if she caught her wearing that disgusting lotion ever again she would personally see to it that she got fired, but she settled for ordering a sparkling water instead. "Please don't call me Ms. Winthrop," she added. "That's my mother."

She heard a shuffling sound behind her and then her name. "Lina." That voice. Mari. "Listen, I know you don't want to talk to me, you're making that pretty clear, but I promise I'll leave you alone if you just . . ."

The bartender reappeared with Lina's drink, and Mari closed her mouth. Lina appreciated the diversion. She took a long sip, resisting the urge to chug the entire glass. Trip's crew burst in from the locker room, their hair dripping wet.

"Hannah! My love!" Trip sang. The bartender's cheeks flushed. "How about a cold one?"

"One *pop* coming right up." Hannah winked, filling a glass with ice.

Lina felt sick to her stomach. As usual the rules didn't apply to the Gregorys. His brother was a murderer, a girl had died—a girl everyone knew and loved—and he was walking around ordering drinks and winking at the staff. Life went on. And Trip joked and flirted his way through it, above it.

Mari cast one last look at Lina, who wiped her eyes furiously. Tears meant weakness and Lina had to be strong. Her dad had taught her that. It was a waste of energy to cry over not making the team or getting dumped or falling down. He wouldn't listen to it. "*Stop crying. Grow up. Walk it off.*" He'd spat the same words at her over the years, and she'd learned to control the feelings that accompanied them. He was right. Tears were worthless. And no matter how intense the pain of losing Willa was, it wouldn't kill her. On the other hand, sitting around watching Trip Gregory order a fresh drink while James replenished his stash of roofies just might.

As Mari tried to duck out of the bar, Trip planted himself in her path. His hand lightly grazed her thigh. Another wave of nausea rolled through Lina, but she reminded herself this was exactly what she needed. Mari's gaze locked on Trip's. He nodded almost imperceptibly. Trip was the kind of guy who lived for taking risks and almost getting caught—or getting caught and facing zero consequences. Then he turned to Lina.

"Dress down day, Lina?" he asked playfully, his eyes wandering over the length of her body.

She clenched her fingers into fists. "Something like that," she replied.

Trip scribbled his signature on the bill charging the Gregory account, slipped down from the stool and was gone. Mari opened her mouth to say something, but eventually sighed and followed him out of the sunroom. From watching the interaction, Lina knew they had made plans to meet. His little nod had said it all. She waited thirty seconds, got up, and casually headed in the same direction.

Sure enough, as Mari passed the men's locker room, Trip ducked out, grabbed her hand, and pulled her in. Lina reminded herself that she didn't give a shit about Mari. But then she thought of how Willa made Lina call her whenever she got home at night after a party, just to let her know she was safe. No one had ever thought to do that before. Lina was pretty sure no one would ever do it again.

She shoved herself into the locker room after them, her body pressed tightly against the navy blue walls. She slipped her phone out of her pocket and hit record, praying the microphone would be sensitive enough to pick up their conversation. She marveled at the décor: all cherry wood and rich granite. While the women's locker room was outdated and shabby, the men's was incredibly expensive and modern. The only thing missing was some kind of phallic monument to really drive the point home. Clearly, here was a place where Hawthorne men could go to feel like true men. Or ravage the staff.

"Are you sure no one's in here? I feel like I just heard something." Mari sounded worried.

"Will you just relax? It's almost dinner. Everyone's starting cocktails." Trip's voice was muffled, probably by his lips on Mari's neck or God only knew where. Lina's lower back began to sweat.

"I just . . ."

Lina could feel a shift in the air, an energy that wasn't there before.

"You just what?" Trip's voice was clipped. "Here . . ." he'd managed to soften it. "This will help you relax."

It didn't take a rocket scientist to imagine what he held out to Mari. No doubt it was tiny and white.

"I don't know. I'm okay. It's fine." Mari laughed uncomfortably.

"Take it." It wasn't a suggestion. Lina pictured Mari's full lips wrapping around the tiny pill, swallowing it dry, submitting to the effects of the drug, to Trip, to it all. And she got pissed. She switched her phone to camera mode and snuck around the corner, taking continuous pictures while trying to block out the images in front of her. The word "victim" came to mind as Trip lay on top of Mari on a narrow wooden bench, Mari who was now listless. Lina felt something twist inside of her. It was like facing her dad's wrath all over again, only this time she relished the pain. Without pain there would be no anger, and without anger there would be no courage. And she was going to need all the courage she could get.

"Stop!" she shouted.

"What the . . . ?" Trip had the decency to appear shocked, at least for a moment. Then he smiled, slow and confident. "Oh, I get it. You want in on this, don't you Lina Ballerina?"

The perversity of Sloane's nickname on his lips made something inside her snap. Without thinking, Lina charged. "Get off of her." She pushed at his pale chest with all of her weight. "Get the hell off."

He laughed clumsily as he fell back on the wood floor. "Relax, Lina. I was kidding." He grabbed his shorts and buttoned them quickly. "But stay out of my business." He gestured loosely at Mari, still collapsed on the bench, "And I'll stay out of yours." He stared at her a few seconds too long, then turned to walk out of the locker room. "Gentlemen's quarters are off limits, Lina Ballerina," he called. "The Captain is going to be pissed. I'd keep a low profile if I were you."

He let the door slam behind him and Lina turned her attention to Mari. She forced herself to focus on her face and ignore the fact that she was laying down, half naked.

"Are you okay?" It was kind of a ridiculous question, but it was the best Lina could do.

Mari didn't respond, just looked up at her with glassy eyes, her expression unreadable.

"Come on, let's get you dressed." Lina tried to grab Mari's limp arms to pull her into a seated position, but her hands were slapped away.

"Get off me. I'm fine." Mari sat up and threw her shirt on over her head.

"But Trip . . . he was just . . ."

"All over me? Yeah. That's kind of the idea, Lina. What do you think I was trying to tell you? What happened on the Fourth, no one can know about it, okay? God, you're worse than Rose."

"Wait, Rose McCaan?"

Lina stood there with her mouth hanging open, phone in hand. Mari and Rose were friends? No wonder Rose had freaked out when Lina mentioned Mari's role in their plan the other night.

Before she could respond, Mari snatched Lina's phone out from her grasp. "Yup, Rose and I go way back." She tossed the phone in her oversized purse and hurried out of the locker room.

Chapter 13

Lina sat on the curb outside of the Club for what felt like forever. Could have been minutes, could have been hours. She didn't know. Didn't really care. She was done fighting. Done walking off the pain. She was ready to wallow. She watched the early birds arrive, white-haired and stooped, helping each other out of their gigantic cars. The twenty-something happy hour crowd came next, the girls sporting spaghetti straps and full faces of makeup, some of the guys wearing suits straight from work. Their entrance was loud, full of life and possibility. Her heart pulled when she saw families arrive a bit later. A group of middle school girls trailed behind their parents with their arms linked. The girl in the middle looked directly at Lina and smiled at her exactly the way Willa used to smile at people who looked lonely.

As they walked into the Club, arms tight, Lina couldn't help but think about how easily they'd break. *Red rover, red rover, let Lina come over.* If the War failed, it was those girls who would suffer. Those girls who would eventually be hurt and taken advantage of by the Gregorys.

"Lina?"

Rose McCaan appeared at the curb. Her long hair was a mess of frizz, and she was wearing the most heinous pair of khaki shorts Lina had ever laid eyes on.

"It should be illegal to have that many pockets," Lina mumbled. What did one put in all of those pockets? Drugs? Phones? Evidence? All of the things Lina was missing. All of the things that Mari had probably given to Rose. Her mind raced with the best way to confront Rose about Mari. She had to be careful. She needed that phone, and until she had it in her hands, she needed Rose, too.

"Nice to see you, too. I've been calling you." Rose shifted her weight from foot to foot like she had to pee. Lina had never met anyone who was so consistently nervous. "Come on. We have to get ready. He's meeting me here. Soon." Rose scowled, waiting for a response. When Lina offered none, she rolled her eyes and started toward the doors. "Pool house in five. If you're not there, I'll just text Madge. She's been looking for you, too, you know."

Shit. Madge. Lina knew she'd want to know exactly what she'd learned about Trip after a long day of stalking. She'd want to see pictures; she'd ask why Lina hadn't called her back. As much as Lina wanted to stay on that curb for the rest of her life, there was no way she was going to tell Madge that she'd messed up everything with Trip. That there was now a waitress walking around Hawthorne Lake reading all of her texts about the War and the Gregorys. Her best bet was to get her phone back and figure out exactly what Mari and Rose were planning together. She had to play along and let Rose screw up first.

Lina hurried after her toward the huge pool behind the Club. By this time, the sun was low in the sky. It couldn't set fast enough, as far as Lina was concerned. A couple sat at the edge, dipping their feet. The rest of the deck was clear. Rose wandered aimlessly, staring at the couple and back to Lina. It would have gone on like that for hours if Lina hadn't intervened.

"You want them to leave I take it?" Lina could feel Rose's eyes examining the colorful tattoos that snaked up and down her arms. She felt like saying, "My eyes are up here," but didn't care enough to bother. She kind of liked being a freak show. Especially to the boring girls like Rose. "Ooh, I know, let's go skinny dipping!" Lina exclaimed loudly. She started to take off her shirt while Rose watched in horror and the woman grabbed her husband by the arm and yanked him inside. "See? Works every time."

"Right, well, it doesn't work for me. I could get in a lot of trouble . . . my mom?" Rose's voice cracked.

Lina felt like punching her. "What's the big plan, so we can both get this over with?" she groaned.

"Plan?" Rose squeaked.

"Uh yeah, you know, how you're planning on getting James naked. How'd you get him here anyway? Promise of a quickie in the locker room?" Lina waited for her to take the bait.

"Yeah . . . um . . . that." Rose stared down at her phone. In a sudden burst of inspiration, Lina stole Mari's move. She almost felt like she was watching someone else as she yanked the phone right out from Rose's grasp. Perfect. She'd use Rose's phone as collateral to get her own phone back. She couldn't believe she hadn't thought of it sooner.

"Hey!" Rose shrieked, lunging at Lina. "You can't? Come on . . ."

But Lina was already three steps ahead of her and faster than Rose. Her sandals clattered on the flagstones as she flipped through the texts. *Oh, my God.* There wasn't a single text from Mari. Instead the phone was full of messages from James. They went back to long before Willa had died. All *pleases* and *forgive mes* and *I need to see yous*.

"You like him." Lina stopped dead in her tracks and whirled around. Her eyes bored into Rose's. "You like him and you're trying to protect him. That's why you joined, isn't it? You wanted to save your psycho killer boyfriend? Well, congratulations. Mission accomplished. For your information, I had everything we needed to get the Gregorys cut off. Everything. And I lost it. Your stupid little friend stole it." Lina laughed bitterly. "So, knock yourself out. None of this even matters. Why don't you go screw your boyfriend, and we can call it a day, 'kay?"

"You bitch."

Lina blinked. It was the first time Lina had ever heard Rose raise her voice. "What did you—"

"You think you're the only one hurting here?" Rose snapped. "I don't see you risking a goddamned thing for Willa. All you had to do was pony up twenty-five thousand dollars. A drop in the bucket for you. I gave up everything for this. My parents. My friends. My . . ." Her voice trailed off and Lina could only guess that James's name was going to come next. "Screw it, keep my phone. The camera is next to the couch if you change your mind." Rose straightened her shoulders and walked back toward the chairs lining the pool deck. "And before you go around saying that none of this matters, remember that we're talking about Willa here. Your best friend. Even I know she was too good a person to let her killer go free."

Lina opened her mouth, but the words caught in her throat. Rose vanished inside. The worst part about Rose's little speech was that she was right. Her knees trembled as she lowered herself into one of the upholstered lounge chairs, her hands useless in her lap. Funny: this was where she first met Willa. This exact spot, on the first day of the Club's summer camp. Dumping your annoying middle school-aged child off at day camp was a time-honored Hawthorne Lake tradition. Lina swore her mother actually swiped her hands together after closing the car door, like Lina were a bag of trash on garbage day. And she kind of was. Glasses, baby fat, braces, and the beginnings of boobs no one bothered to help fit for a bra. If it weren't for the incessant name calling at her school, Lina would still stink to high heaven, but she'd at least learned to sneak her mom's deodorant.

And then she had seen Willa. Beautiful, even at an age where nobody was. Willa, who didn't have to suffer through braces or get made fun of for having a mustache or bad eyebrows or zits or any of the other requisite humiliations of puberty: always the girl everyone wished they could be. And when Willa saw her that was it: she chose Lina to be her friend. No strings attached. There wasn't some glamorous makeover, a dramatic unveiling of contacts and a cut and color all thanks to the beautiful blonde taking pity on the ugly duckling. There was just friendship. And fun. It was the first time Lina ever remembered anyone really liking her for who she really was. Honestly, it might have been the last.

"What the hell have I done?" she whispered out loud.

She had been wrong about Rose. She wanted Rose to have an agenda so she'd have a reason to hate her. A reason that wasn't based on petty jealousy.

Lina pushed herself to her feet. She didn't head to the pool house because she felt bad for misjudging Rose. She didn't go to prove to herself that losing Willa hadn't turned her into a jealous bitch. No, Lina went to the pool house because all those years ago Willa had picked her. And when she crouched beside a leather chair and balanced herself on the terracotta tiles, her fingers tight on the camera, she was determined to finally take a real risk in return.

Lina paced the small shadowy pool house. Dusk had now fully settled in. The pool lights clicked on, and the water glowed like turquoise glass against the dark stone of the deck. Soon, couples would begin to spill out from within the Club, second and third glasses of wine in hand. Lina chewed her lip. Time wasn't on her and Rose's side. But then she heard a shatter. Where James Gregory walked, the sound of breaking glass inevitably followed. He was good at breaking things.

Rose froze, and even in the dark Lina saw her eyes widen. She was scared. Lina never should have agreed to let Rose do the dirty work. There was just no way in hell Ms. Stick-Up-Her-Ass was ever going to have the balls to get James naked. In poured James like the alcohol he was so fond of. He practically fell into the pool area, stumbled over the threshold, barely able to right himself. Brown liquid sloshed over the rim of his glass, his sunglasses perched at the end of his nose even though the day was long over. His eyes landed on Rose above his sunglasses, and he straightened, lunging in her direction.

Rose's first instinct seemed to be to take a step backward, but she quickly ducked around him and spun toward the pool, reversing places as if they were doing some sort of messed-up tango. Lina's stomach clenched. She resisted the urge to scream at Rose to stop, that he was dangerous, that he was drunk, that it could happen again. But she was right here this time. She was in control. She could save Rose if she needed saving.

"Hey." Rose said the word softly, like an invitation,

"I've tried calling you so many times. You never pick up. Never. What are you, scared?" James lurched toward her again.

Warning bells sounded in Lina's ears. This was not going to end well. But she stayed where she was with her camera trained on the two of them.

Rose paused and shook her head slowly. "Not scared. Not exactly."

"Well, you should be. You need to stay the hell away from me. Everyone does."

"But it was supposed to be me." Rose said the words so quietly that Lina almost missed them. "I was supposed to be with you that night. Not Willa."

James let out a short bark of laughter. "Oh! So you have a death wish? That's why you're talking to me all of the s-s-sudden." He slurred his words. "It's all coming together now."

Rose spun and bolted.

Lina ducked down, fiddling with the camera to turn it off. Her hands trembled. Enough was enough. She had no desire to watch two attempted date rapes in one day. The red light of the camera finally blinked off. She started toward the pool house door. This tango was over. But by the time Lina made it out to the pool, James was collapsed at Rose's feet. She scowled at Rose.

"He fell. Tripped over one of the chairs. And now he's out." Rose kneeled down and started unbuttoning his shirt while Lina stood there gaping at her. A pool umbrella lay beside James's limp body. Either it had fallen from the table a good ten feet away or someone had grabbed it. "Well? What are you waiting for? This is it. Get the camera."

"Did you . . . ?" She wanted to ask Rose if she'd hit James with the umbrella. She wanted to apologize for being such a bitch and questioning her loyalty to Willa. She wanted to thank her for being able to fix the mess Lina had made of this entire day, but instead, she obeyed Rose's order without so much as a peep. It was the best Lina could do. Besides, these pictures? They were going to be worth way more than any of her words.

Chapter 14

For the first time in a long while, Lina woke up without the feeling of dread heavy on her chest. It took her eyes a second to adjust to the morning light filtering in through her blinds. Her entire back wall, crown molding to baseboard, was covered in photographs. Most were from school, her friends bunched together with arms slung around shoulders, smiles so big they threatened to take over entire faces, wearing everyone's clothes but their own. And then there was summer. Hawthorne Lake, bikinis, sunshine, and beach parties. Early lunches, late dinners, illicit happy hours. Home. Madge, Sloane and . . . Willa.

Lina's smile vanished. She shot up in bed, her hands reaching for her neck, gasping for air as if ripping a hole in her throat might help her breathe. But it was no use. At least she'd had a few minutes of happiness this morning. That was longer than she'd had in ages.

The girls were due to meet at their usual spot in the Club's attic, and because Rose kicked ass last night, Lina actually had something to show for an otherwise waste of a day. So strange: the only thing Lina had been right about when it came to Rose McCaan was her atrocious fashion sense. The girl had proved herself and beyond.

Lina slipped into a fitted cotton dress—it skimmed her mid-thigh—and a pair of wedges that added more height to her already statuesque frame. Every single psychiatrist she was forced to talk to told her she was obsessed with her appearance to compensate for feeling like an outcast as a kid. After the third lecture, she got her first tattoo. It hurt like a bitch, but the shock on her shrink's face had made it completely worthwhile.

When she raced into the attic, breathless to see the look on Madge's face at the pictures they'd taken of James last night, Rose was the only one waiting. Her hair had frizzed into a comically large halo around her head. In her defense, it was about a million degrees up there. Lina touched her closely cropped hair to make sure it hadn't curled in the heat. Nope. Straight as a bone, as always. This is why God invented hot irons and hair product.

"Where is everyone? I skipped coffee."

"Good morning, sunshine," Rose quipped.

Lina raised her eyebrows. And smiled. Briefly. She didn't want to give Rose any ideas. Respect and friendship were two very different things.

"They're running late. Didn't you see the texts?"

Lina flushed. "Oh . . . um, yeah. My battery totally died yesterday. I have to go to the store today to get a new one," she finished lamely. She had mentally ticked off a list of excuses about her phone in bed last night, and this one had sounded a lot better in her head. Oh well. She'd find Mari and figure everything out right after the meeting. The other girls would never have to know.

"So, how'd I do?" Lina gestured to the array of photographs spread across the old table, private-investigator style. "You know I got an A plus in photography last year."

"We did well. Really well," Rose said, smiling. "Took me all night, and I nearly broke my dad's laser printer." Lina never realized how pretty Rose could be. Her dimpled cheeks practically glowed. With the right clothes and makeup, she might even pass for a Club member. "I mean, look at this level of detail."

Lina bent down beside Rose, tucking her legs beneath her, their heads almost touching. She couldn't believe how realistic the pictures looked. The angle made James appear fully naked. Rose had photoshopped her bathing suit from her body, had changed her dark hair to red and strategically arranged the strands so they covered her face. Lina wasn't sure how much more incriminating you could get. With the Club pool in the background, James might as well have been giving his Grandpa the finger. Photoshopped or not, Lina couldn't imagine how much Rose was risking by lying next to James with her bare back to the camera. If that didn't demonstrate her loyalty to the girls, she wasn't sure what would. "You look hot, Rose. You need to save these. They could come in handy if you ever need something more than a headshot."

Rose laughed so hard she snorted. Lina lost it, too. Laughter echoed off the walls, tears gathered in her eyes. Lina couldn't remember the last time her stomach muscles had ached from anything besides an ab workout.

"Something funny?"

Madge stood in the doorway. Lina wiped her eyes, and Rose stiffened like they'd been caught making out.

"Nothing, we were just admiring my wicked photo skills," Lina said, bending to pick up a picture and hand it to Madge. She smiled proudly. Sloane entered behind Madge with a tray of coffees, barely looking at her. She was still pissed about the other day, not that Lina could blame her. Unfortunately, she had no idea how to fix it. She also knew Sloane well enough to know that she would now feel threatened by Rose. "You look pretty, Sloane. You haven't worn your hair down in a while." Sloane's long black hair hung down her back like a curtain, all gloss despite the humidity.

"Thanks," Sloane said, shifting the tray to her other hand. Lina could tell that she wanted a reason to stop fighting. "Coffee?" She might as well have said, "Truce?"

Warmth flooded through Lina's body. Coffee and her best friend. It was a good morning. She almost said as much, but then she remembered. Willa. Willa was dead. There was no such thing as a good morning anymore.

Madge sunk into the couch, examining every inch of the photograph. "This is pretty good." Weak enthusiasm, but they were talking about Madge here. She'd sooner slit your throat than gush. "Rose, you can sneak this into the presentation, right?"

"I think so. My mom is clueless with PowerPoint so one of the college kids always puts it together for her. I'll volunteer this year. She's always bugging me to help her out."

Madge nodded her head, pleased. "Lina?" She raised her eyebrows. "What about Trip?"

"Oh, I almost forgot." Sloane set her coffee down and pulled a piece of folded white paper from her pocket. "They gave this to me in the office. It's a message for you, Lina."

Puzzled, she turned around and unfolded the note.

If you want your phone, meet me at the ninth hole. Midnight.

Mari. Of course. The girl was ruining her life, and now she wanted to meet on the freaking golf course like some sting operation? Rose was staring so she quickly shoved the paper into her pocket.

"Trust me, I've got it taken care of," Lina answered with confidence. She'd get her damn phone back, and they would destroy the Gregorys as planned, one incriminating picture at a time. It shouldn't be hard to shut Mari up. Particularly with the safety deposit box at her disposal. She twisted her War key. "I just might need to make a tiny withdrawal from our account to make it happen."

"How much do you need?" Madge narrowed her eyes. Lina regretted accusing Madge of being cheap back in sunnier times. She was careful with money.

"Um, I don't know, like five thousand dollars?"

"Really? That much? What's it for?"

Lina was kicking herself for asking for that much. Five hundred probably would have been enough to pay off Mari to get her phone back. She should have known that anything over a few hundred bucks would lead to questions. "Um, I saw something at the basketball courts, and I think if I can pay off one of the waiters, this will be huge. I mean, that's what the money's for, right? I do have pictures, but this other guy was taking video when it all went down at the courts and video will be more . . ." Lina searched for the right word. The word that would make Madge buy into her bullshit. "Damning. The video will be more damning for sure." *Jesus.* She sounded like someone on one of those stupid crime shows. "I just don't want to jinx it by going into too much detail."

Madge fished her necklace out from under her tank top and wrapped the chain around her finger. "I guess." Lina let herself exhale. "But it better be good. Remember, we need to destroy *both* of them. Everything that happened to Willa is just as much Trip's fault as it is James's."

"Trust me. It's good." Lina forced herself to look into Madge's eyes. It should have been easy because she was telling the truth. The stuff she had on Trip and James wasn't just good. It was amazing. But it didn't change the fact that she had lost all of it when she'd let Mari walk away with her phone. Just thinking about it made her stomach churn as they made their way down the stairs and out to the pool.

It was weird to wish a summer day away. She remembered lying at the pool last summer with Willa, Madge, and Sloane, pulling her string bikini straps down because the only thing that could ruin an afternoon at the Club would have been wonky tan lines. Last year she didn't give a shit if her parents were never around, if she went to bed alone and woke up in an empty house. It was almost easier not to have to answer to anybody. If she could stop time, press pause and soak up all the happy feelings those summer days offered, bask in them like the hot summer sun, she would. But when Willa died it felt like the sun had gone with her, had disappeared behind a wall of clouds. Lina was beginning to think she'd never feel that warmth on her shoulders again.

But they went through the motions. They tanned and swam and pretended to be okay under the watchful eyes of the adults (all except her own parents, of course) in their wide-brimmed sun hats. There was lunch with Madge, dinner with Sloane and her family. And that night, when she slipped under the opening garage door and back into her house, it was just as quiet as she'd left it in the morning. Jodweiga, her housekeeper/glorified nanny, had long ago stopped waiting up for her, so Lina watched mindless television, listened to music too loud, and tried to force the hands of the clock to spin wildly around so it would be time for her to return to the Club to confront the crazy bitch who stole her phone.

Around 11:45 P.M., Lina buttoned her jeans, her tired eyes heavy. She reminded herself how lucky she was. No prying mom or dad to make sure she didn't sneak out at night. Lucky Lina.

The Club looked different when closed, the normally bright windows black against the vine-covered building. Even though she was a member, she was trespassing. She shivered at the thought, wishing she'd remembered to grab a sweater. She forgot how cold it got so close to the lake. And then it occurred to her that she hadn't been this close to the lake at night since Willa died.

She stopped walking, paralyzed by the expanse of liquid black. *I'm panicking.* She knew the feeling, the tightening of her muscles, the familiar constriction of her chest. She needed to sit down, to submit to the attack and let it sink its claws in, only then would it pass. Lina slumped downward, pulling her knees to her chest. She knew it was past midnight. She wasn't even close to the ninth hole, and Mari didn't exactly seem like the patient type.

"You're late." Mari appeared out of thin air, doing nothing to still Lina's already pounding heart. She continued to focus on filling her lungs with air, letting the breath out slowly, and then repeating the process. Lina hated herself for her weakness, for her position below Mari, for not being able to stand tall and control her body. And she hated Mari for being here to witness it. But she gripped the cool grass between her fingers, and pushed herself to her knees. With another breath, she stood a bit wobbly—though taller than Mari, at least.

"Give me . . ." Lina continued to wheeze, her heart slamming in her chest, ". . . my phone."

Mari reached into her bag and calmly placed the phone in Lina's hand. She pulled her eyebrows together. "Are you okay to get yourself home? It seemed like you were having a moment."

"Wait. That's it?" Lina said, finding her voice and breath at the same time. "You take my phone for twenty-four hours and just hand it back over?"

Mari laughed. "I actually should thank you. I should have said that first. Thank you."

Lina pursed her lips, grateful that her panic attack had passed because she was about to burst. "Oh, that's it? Thank me? For what? Trying to stop someone from raping you? Witnessing you willingly taking some date rape drug because Trip Gregory tells you to?" By now Lina was sweating, the earlier chill long forgotten. "Do you want to end up like her?" Her eyes filled with tears as she gestured to the lake. "Do you?"

"You know, it's not always about you. The world doesn't revolve around you and your friends even though I'm sure your mommy and daddy pay a lot of money to make it feel that way." Mari shook her head angrily. "I never take his stupid pills. I never do anything I don't want to do. And I sure as hell don't need to be saved. I had him right where I wanted him the entire time."

"But, you were drugged; you were attacked."

"I was acting. The Gregorys are so easy." Mari leaned in so close that her warm breath tickled Lina's ear. "But then you swooped in to save me." A tiny thrill ran up Lina's spine and she shivered. "Thank you, Lina, for giving me everything that I need." Mari turned to leave, her hair swinging over her shoulder.

The spell was broken. Lina felt like she was going to be

sick. "Wait! You can't tell them what we're doing. You can't do anything with those pictures. You'll ruin us, you'll ruin everything!" She rushed after Mari, grabbing the soft skin of her bicep.

Mari whirled around to face Lina, shaking her loose. Inches away. Close enough for a fight. Close enough for a kiss. "You should actually be thanking me. You dodged a bullet, really. Wouldn't you rather I go to the Captain than tell your parents what happened on the boat?" Mari flashed a dazzling smile, her eyes like knives. "You, Lina, were my Plan B. Lucky for you the Captain pays very well for this kind of information. Your little scheme is going to put me through college."

And all at once Lina understood. Mari was using her, playing her exactly the way she'd played Trip. And worse, she'd bought it. Just like a Gregory. Lucky, lucky, Lina.

Mari started walking back toward the clubhouse. And that's when it hit Lina. If she'd bought it just like a Gregory, she could stop it just like a Gregory.

"The Captain doesn't always pay, you know. But we're a sure thing."

Mari stopped and turned. "You don't have access to that kind of money." There was a note of challenge in her voice. A trace of a dare.

"How does five thousand dollars sound? That ought to cover tuition to whatever crap school you're going to next year."

Mari laughed wickedly. "Make it thirty. Just in case my scholarship falls through."

Shit. Madge was going to kill her if she agreed to pay Mari that much money, but how could she not? Without it they had nothing on Trip and nothing on James beyond Rose's photos. Those weren't going to be enough. Not to destroy the family. Not to win the War.

So Lina nodded her assent and watched Mari disappear back into the night. Everyone had an angle. Everyone had a price. At Hawthorne Lake, life was an auction. The prize always went to the highest bidder.

Chapter 15

The next morning Lina awoke to an earsplitting stream of Polish words. Swearing, probably.

"You gone all night! What I tell your parents?" Jodweiga shrieked. She stormed across Lina's room, her apron tight across her huge belly, throwing open the blinds, picking up discarded bras and bathing suits and hurtling them into the hamper. "They come home in ten minutes. Up! Up!"

Ten minutes? Her parents? This was not good news. Especially since she hadn't fallen asleep until the first rays of sunlight had stabbed through her blinds. Her mind was fuzzy with sleep, still processing everything that had happened with Mari. $30,000. She had twenty-four hours to get Mari the cash before she went to the Captain. Madge was going to kill her. But there was no choice. The stuff on her phone was incriminating enough to get the Gregorys disinherited. It had to be. Plus, it's not like they had anything else to do with the money.

Lina had to get out of the house before her parents arrived. It was already past 11 A.M. The girls would be at the Club plotting, waiting for the evidence she promised them. Her parents would just slow her down with their disappointed sighs and uncomfortable silence. They'd swooped in for Willa's memorial and put on their usual show only to breeze back out just as fast as they'd come. Lina didn't care. She didn't need them pretending to care. It only reminded her of all the things she didn't have.

"*Szybciej*! *Szybciej*! They are here!" Jodweiga ran out of her room to get the rest of the house in order. Car doors slammed. The garage door opened. Footsteps on the stairwell. Lina stood, paralyzed.

Moments later Lina's mother breezed into her room looking like an ad for expensive sportswear.

So much for her escape.

"Lina! Darling! We're home!" Her mother always spoke in exclamation marks. Lina sometimes wondered if that was because she was perpetually surprised by the bullshit that came out of her own mouth. "We've missed you so much! We really wanted to be home more this summer . . . for . . . you know . . ." Her mother lowered her voice when referring to all the things they didn't talk about. "But you know Daddy! Business first!"

"So he got a new secretary?" Lina asked.

"How did you know?" Because even though they'd never admit it, "business first" really meant that her father was screwing his new mistress. Just like "boarding school" was really code for "we want nothing to do with this hot mess of a teenager" and Jodweiga's real job description should have been rent-a-mom. No, there was nothing quite like the Winthrop family's secret dialect heavily rooted in passive aggression with a slight accent of I-don't-give-a-shit.

"Well! Time for breakfast! Jodweiga is getting everything

ready for eggs benny downstairs! Your favorite!" She paused in the doorway.

Lina hadn't eaten eggs Benedict since she was nine years old. They'd been at the Club. Lina scooped up her first bite, the creamy egg dripping with butter and hollandaise sauce, when she'd heard laughing from the corner. One of the servers whispered to another how the fat kid had just ordered a breakfast that clocked in at more than two thousand calories. Lina lost her appetite for eggs Benedict after that. Now she stuck to the fruit plate.

"I'm not hungry. I'm supposed to meet Madge at the Club."

"Don't be silly! Besides, I'm not asking, I'm telling." Her mother's smile darkened. Lina knew there was no point in arguing. "Now, darling, go ahead and get dressed. Perhaps something with sleeves! As much as your father enjoys seeing your rather unusual form of self-expression," her mother nodded at the rainbow of ink running like ivy up her arms, "I think we can all agree those *things* are best left unseen until after coffee."

Her mother swept back down the stairs leaving only a cloud of her expensive perfume in her wake. In a few days, that's all that would be left of her, Lina reminded herself. But she still mourned the loss of a deserted house and the freedom that came with it.

She pulled on her bikini and threw a bright yellow, long sleeved dress over her head. Even in the air conditioning, the light cotton material clung to her arms and she longed for one of her spaghetti strapped cover ups. But her mother was right. Reminding her father of her rebellion would only delay her departure to the Club. She ran down the stairs to find her parents already seated at the enormous dining room table.

Her father was buried behind *The Wall Street Journal*. Classic. *Nice to see you again, too, Dad. How long has it been?* She slid into her designated seat.

"Lina darling, don't you look becoming! That color really suits you! Doesn't she look lovely, Martin?"

"Good morning, Carolina." Her dad cast a quick scrutinizing gaze from over the top of the page.

"Well! Let's eat, shall we?" Lina's mother whipped open her cloth napkin and started placing delicate bites of egg whites onto her tongue. Lina pushed her eggs Benedict around on the plate. There was no way in hell she was going to eat a single bite, but maybe if she pushed it around enough her parents wouldn't notice.

Her father tucked away his newspaper and took a long sip of coffee.

"So, Carolina, your mother and I understand that this summer has been . . . difficult." He cleared his throat. "But . . ." *You are a waste. You are a disappointment. We don't give a shit.* Lina could think of an infinite number of words to fill her father's pause. "Have you managed to find a productive use of your time?"

"Well, that depends, Dad. Do you consider hanging out with my friends at the pool to be productive?"

Her father frowned, deep creases forming around his lips. "I thought we'd discussed you getting an internship. Learning something about the world."

Lina felt like reminding her dad that they never discussed anything. Ever. So he must be hallucinating or perhaps thinking of some other daughter he had squirreled away with one of his secretaries. Instead she continued to push the congealing eggs Benedict.

"Well! I'm sure your friends need you right now after

everything with Willa." Her mother's bright smile belied the seriousness of her statement. "How is Madge doing?" She asked the question like a news anchor bantering with a guest.

"She's fine, Mom." Lina stood up and pushed her plate away. This torture had gone on long enough. "Speaking of Madge, I'm late. She's waiting for me at the Club. I'll see you guys later."

"Sit down, Carolina. You haven't even touched your food." Her father's eyes were sharp, the frown lines slicing his square jaw.

"I'm not hungry."

"You're not going anywhere until you eat." He cleared his throat and finally put the paper down. "We're trying to be patient, you know."

Without breaking eye contact, Lina sat back down and shoveled eggs Benedict in her mouth. It was cold and the sauce had congealed into clumps of fat, but she barely noticed because she didn't bother chewing, just swallowed the eggs. Soggy pieces of English muffin stuck in her throat. She choked it all down, her watery eyes never once leaving her father's.

"There. Done." Her mother's face had gone slack, her father's red with anger. For a second he looked like he was going to say something important. Something real.

But Jodweiga cleared her throat and gestured at Lina's plate. "You finish?" By the time Lina had nodded and Jodweiga had left, her father's eyes had wandered again to the newsprint. That was exactly how much he cared. The realization should have hurt, but Lina was past all that. She almost felt bad for her mother, staring at him, willing him to look at her. And Lina realized that was exactly what James Gregory and Willa Ames-Rowan might have looked like in twenty years if everything had gone according to plan.

A wave of dizziness crashed over her. Lina's worlds were blending and bleeding together, the lines becoming hazy. They were generations apart, but they were all the same. She might not be able to save her mom, but she could save herself and her daughter and her daughter's daughter. And it had to start here. Now. All roads led to the War, and that's exactly where Lina was headed in her tiny convertible.

Well, right after she stopped at the bank to grab $30,000 from their safety deposit box.

Chapter 16

"You gave your mom the file, right?" Madge asked Rose for what had to be the millionth time.

They'd just completed the presentation that morning. Lina felt confident, all things considered. It was nearly perfect. All sickly, wild-eyed, desperate-looking kids intermixed with flashes of naked Gregorys and grainy pictures of discreet drug deals. It was so entirely wrong, so sad and twisted, that Lina knew without a shadow of a doubt that it was going to work. And now it was show time.

She watched the parade of ancient gala women, dresses too short, waltz through the Club's main doors. Botox, boobs, and bitches: the Club trifecta. She wondered if the horror would even show on their smooth, surgically frozen faces when they viewed the corrupted slides. The Captain's neck would turn an angry red when his shame and revulsion became too much to bear. Lina wondered if she'd be able to see the exact moment the boys were disinherited, if she'd bear witness to the historic event. She'd be watching for it.

Of course there was someone else she'd have to watch out for tonight: Mari. A bubble of uncertainty rose up in Lina's throat. She closed her eyes and reminded herself that as long as everything went as planned she'd have no problem silencing Mari. Madge wouldn't care about all that money as long as the Gregorys were destroyed. That was the goal. That was what Lina needed to be focusing on right now.

"Your mom really has no idea?" Madge asked.

"No," Rose murmured, her patience wearing thin. "She was just thrilled I actually helped her, and that I know Power-Point. It's all cued up and ready to roll."

Madge nodded and headed into the courtyard, Sloane on her heels.

Lina paused for a second with Rose.

Hawthorne Lake Country Club was bathed in white. Creamy linens were draped over tables and chairs; lights sparkled from every tree; hundreds of white hydrangeas, snapdragons, and roses were bunched in vases on every available surface. But the most spectacular addition to the theatrics was the clear surface suspended over the pool, the tables situated on top, as if floating over the glowing water. All of the guests were required to wear white. Maybe someone believed it could be like fresh snow in a city, covering up the dirt and sludge, transforming sin to purity. Still, even though Lina knew exactly what lurked beneath the surface, she had to admit that it was stunning. The Captain had truly outdone himself this year, and she almost hated to ruin it. Almost.

Soon, an orchestra of overlapping conversations mixed with clinking wine glasses, punctuated every so often by the pop of a champagne bottle. The Captain was in his element. His laugh rained down upon the crowd, rivaled only by Trip's. Even though the Captain acted as though

Trip didn't exist, the two were so similar. They glowed and preened in the spotlight, while James, the Captain's favorite, lurked around the edges. She caught him exchanging harsh words with his brother. Trip's eyes glazed over as James spoke, wandering in search of someone more important. She knew it was only a matter of time before someone slapped his back and he turned, leaving James to choke on whatever he wanted to communicate. It was the same exact thing her father did to her at breakfast, the same thing he did to her every time she said something that he didn't agree with. Before she could stop herself, Lina felt sorry for James. And almost as instantaneously, she hated herself for it.

"Should we mingle?" Rose asked. Lina couldn't determine if she was frightened or sarcastic.

Lina glanced at her. Rose wore an unflattering white dress, the high neckline doing nothing for her boobs, which were shoved in and flattened together like one large, lumpy pancake. Lina would have liked nothing more than to load the both of them into her car and head back to her closet where she had an airy sundress with a sweetheart neckline that would make Rose look like Sophia Loren. Willa would have approved. Instead, Lina grabbed Rose's arm to yank her into the bathroom. They might not have time for a full makeover but surely she could do something about those boobs.

"Wait. My mom needs me. We'll talk after." Rose shot her an apologetic look and made her way over to her mother's side. Not for the first time, Lina wondered if Pilar would be fired over what was about to happen. The girls hadn't discussed that possibility, but she was surprised Rose hadn't brought it up. She knew her family probably needed the money. Then again, Rose always seemed to be surprising Lina.

Sloane looked bored, fawned over by her parents, who

showed her off proudly. She kept rolling her eyes at Lina, who scanned the courtyard for Madge. At least Madge was parentless tonight, too. Lina hated herself for thinking it, but it was true. Mr. and Mrs. Ames-Rowan had never missed a gala. Their absence and their surviving daughter's atten-dance served as a reminder of Willa's death, the one thing every single person at the Club was actively trying to forget. Because when it came down to it, they were all guilty. Every single person who was in the tent that night had also been on the yacht. And every single one of them had let James Gregory get away with murder. They might as well have driven the getaway car.

Finally she spotted Madge, alone in a corner.

As hard as these beautiful people tried to forget, tried to move on, tried to feign innocence, not one of them could bear to look at Madge. Lina wondered if it hurt to be ignored. But Madge sat almost painfully straight in her chair, a careful half smile on her face. If her demotion from Club darling to Club pariah stung, she didn't let it show. Lina walked over and settled in next to her friend, resisting the urge to hug her close.

"Five minutes," Madge whispered, her eyes fixed on the presentation screen. Maybe she was too busy with the War to notice anyone not noticing her. It wasn't the same for Lina. Practically everywhere she went, she was noticed. If not for her sharp cheekbones and the graceful curve of her lips, then the shocking tattoos decorating her body. She was identified as "that tall girl" or "the pretty one" or if the person doing the identifying were a woman over forty, "the one with those *tattoos*." Tonight was no different.

The squeal of a microphone tore Lina from her thoughts. The Captain appeared at the podium in front of the screen.

Lina's heart pounded, the pulse in her ears drowning out his words. He gave his usual speech about the power of community and generosity of Hawthorne Lake's members. It was because of the Club that the children at St. Anthony's Children's Hospital were receiving a new multimillion-dollar art wing. The subtext? We at the Club have already moved beyond the charity created in Willa's name. There's no need to remember her. We have a new reason to pat ourselves on the back. As she watched the Captain speak, the entire audience hanging on each and every word, electricity coursed through Lina's body. This was it. In a few minutes, the Gregorys would be destroyed.

The presentation began. Madge leaned forward in her seat. Sloane had broken away from her parents, and Rose pulled back from her mom. Lina imagined they wanted some distance to enjoy the show. Rose caught Lina's eye, offering a hesitant smile, and for the first time, without even thinking, Lina returned it. A picture of a Disney starlet and a little boy in a hospital bed, tubes connected every which way, filled the screen. Lina knew what came next. She held her breath.

And there it was. The first picture. The $30,000 shot. Trip groping Mari in the locker room.

A hush fell over the crowd; women slapped hands over their mouths; men straightened. The Captain frowned at the silence that had spread over the room like a cloak. And he turned to the screen just in time to see old Trip up to no good. And then another picture of a sick child filled the screen, this one with a baseball cap on that did nothing to disguise the slashes of purple beneath the child's eyes. Before the Captain could wonder if perhaps the image was a trick of the light, a figment of his imagination, James was next. His long torso, completely nude, covered by a photoshopped Rose. The Captain slowly lowered his drink.

"What the hell is this? Pilar! Turn this off. Immediately."

He stood in front of the projector and tried to block an image of the drug deal with his broad shoulders. Pilar, incredibly ungraceful under pressure, bent behind the computer, pressing buttons and pulling cords, managing only to raise the volume on the presentation. Trip had the sense to appear stunned and James stared at the screen, his body rigid, his face stoic. With a desperate yank, Pilar pulled the plug, and the screen went black. But it was too late. Lina lowered herself back in her seat to watch the Captain, waiting for the moment.

He shook his head slowly for what felt like hours. And then he spoke.

"I apologize for that rather inappropriate disruption," the Captain said rubbing his jaw with his hand. "It appears that my grandsons are having a bit of fun with their grandfather, and you all had the privilege of witnessing their little practical joke." Trip tried to laugh it off, but his cheeks were too red. James just stalked away from the pool, his arm knocking into an empty chair making it wobble on its feet. The Captain continued to shake his head, and Lina wondered if he was going to disown the boys publicly, cutting them off in front of everyone as she hoped. She wanted to see Trip's face when his party was broken up, she wanted to watch James punch something, wanted to see the boys unravel.

But when the Captain lifted his eyes back to the crowd, they were a softer shade of blue and one side of his lip twitched. If Lina didn't know better, she'd say he was about to laugh. Was he? Madge stiffened, shaking her own head back and forth, confirming Lina's suspicion. And then the Captain smiled. It was a moment all right. Just not the one she'd been waiting for. "But let's not allow this joke to ruin the evening. After all, you know what they say, 'boys will be boys.'" He winked at the crowd and some of the men chuckled. Most women still appeared a bit stunned. But no one said anything; no one called anyone out; no one voiced an opinion, if they even had one. Madge sat completely still, her hands shaking with barely suppressed rage.

"These boys keep me young," the Captain continued. "But make no mistake. I taught them everything they know."

This time a few women laughed, too. Bile rose in Lina's throat making her cough.

"Your salads will be arriving shortly and after dinner, we'll head to the ballroom for the silent auction. Enjoy!" And that was it.

Trip's friends slapped his back. Salads were placed on tables and red wine poured into glasses. James had disappeared.

"This isn't over." Madge whispered the words so only Lina could hear, a bland smile plastered on her face. Lina scanned the crowd for the remaining girls. Rose stared at the screen her face blank with shock. Sloane's eyes fell on Lina, tears glittering above her lashes. It was almost as if Willa had died all over again. Just like on the Fourth of July, their hands were bound, mouths sealed shut, the fight siphoned from them like gas from a rusty car. Lina's phone buzzed in her clutch. Mari. She wanted her money. A wave of dizziness passed over her and she swayed dangerously in her chair. All of the hope she'd built up over the past few days had been snuffed out.

Lina shoved out from behind her chair and made a beeline for the golf course.

"Lina, wait!" Rose called after her.

But Lina ran—out of the patio, away from the sea of glittering white and chattering voices. How could she have been so stupid? Did she really believe she and her friends would have a chance against the Gregorys? She couldn't bear to think about what would happen if Mari told the Captain who was behind those pictures. Some juvenile detention facility? Military school? By the time she found Mari sitting in front of the pin, ashing her cigarette into the hole, Lina was barefoot and tear streaked. She wasn't sure when she'd begun crying, but now she couldn't seem to stop.

"Here." She tossed the roll of bills in Mari's direction. "Take your damn money."

Mari flipped through the bills and looked up at Lina from beneath her heavy lashes.

"I could have sworn we said sixty."

"You're out of your mind. Take it and get the hell out of here. I never want to see you again."

"You sure about that? I mean, I don't want to be a tattletale or anything, but I'm guessing your dad would be pretty pissed off if he knew about his only daughter's sexual tendencies."

"I don't . . ." Lina tried to find the words, but the denial died on her lips. Who the hell was she kidding?

"You're not getting a penny over whatever she just gave you." Rose's voice was clear and strong in the night.

Mari was on her feet and in Rose's face in one fluid motion. "Oh look, you decided to become a maid to the little rich girls after all. Your mother must be so proud." The key on Rose's necklace caught in the moonlight. Mari lifted it off Rose's chest. "Your friend over here has the same one, doesn't she? Does that make you her bitch now?"

"I'd rather be her bitch than the Gregorys' whore."

For a second Lina thought she must have heard wrong.

Mari took a step backward and dropped her cigarette.

"Fine. I'll keep your secrets so you can keep telling the same old lies. But eventually you'll realize that the whores are the only women winning in this place." Mari flashed her icy smile. "At least we're getting paid."

Lina watched as Mari stuffed the money into her pocket and walked toward the lake.

"How much did you give her?" Rose asked.

"Thirty thousand." Lina shook her head and wiped at the tears on her cheeks. "Madge is going to kill me."

"Us," Rose said softly. "She's going to kill us."

"No, it's my fault. We had this . . . thing . . . on the Fourth and then she stole my phone and . . ."

"Are you sure?" Rose interrupted Lina. "Because I think I might have been the one who left it at the pool the other night."

Lina stared at Rose for a beat before she realized that she'd never be able to get the words out. So instead of saying thank you, she did what Willa would have done. She linked her arm through Rose's and walked her friend back to the Club.

Lina scanned the crowded deck at the party. Her eyes caught on a couple near the stern who were lost in each other. A mess of hands and lips and tangled limbs.

"Whoa, get a room Piper Worthington." Willa sidled up next to her, laughing.

"Aw, don't be mean. She's just trying to fit in now that Alexander dumped her." Sloane's forehead creased with sympathy.

"Whatever," Lina muttered. "She reeks of eau de desperate and you know it." But she couldn't keep the jealousy from her voice.

"You know you could have him, right? Any of them. All you'd have to do is snap your fingers." Willa hooked her arm into the crook of Lina's. Sloane nodded enthusiastically beside her. Sloane probably thought she was helping Willa make Lina feel better. Of course she did.

"Why ladies," Lina batted lashes heavy with mascara, "haven't you heard the rumors? I've already had them all."

"I believe what I see, Lina Ballerina." Willa gave her a look that said too much. Lina's stomach knotted.

"Well then, watch this." Lina grabbed a guy talking to a group of girls opposite them. She whirled him around and snaked her arms around his neck.

"Hi." She breathed, her voice soft and sexy. The voice she practiced in the mirror at night.

"Whoa."

Stale vodka breath washed over her face. Her new friend had clearly had one drink too many, but that didn't matter. Not now. Not to Lina. She pressed her lips against his. They were wet and soft, like slugs. He tasted of alcohol and cigarettes. Lina's first instinct was to gag and pull away, but she forced herself further into his embrace, using her tongue to gently open his mouth, willing herself to feel the warm ache that her friends described when they kissed boys.

But there was nothing. As usual Lina was numb.

He pulled away from her. "Um, I have a girlfriend, so . . . ."

"Right. Well, if you don't tell, I won't." Lina laughed even though she felt like crying.

Willa was still standing a couple feet away, watching her carefully.

The boy stumbled away, shaking his head.

"You know you don't have to do that. We don't care how many guys you kiss, Lina." Willa put her hand on her shoulder and looked her friend directly in the eye. Lina turned away from the piercing blue. Sometimes Willa not only said too much with her gaze, but she saw too much as well. More than Lina wanted her to see.

"It's just a game though, right, Lina?" The hopefulness in Sloane's voice made Lina want to cry. The worst part was that Sloane was right. It was a game to Lina, just a different one than her friend thought she was playing.

"I . . . um . . . I have to pee. I'll be back."

Lina ducked away from the girls and headed toward the stairs. She felt better after escaping the crush of people on the deck; it was calmer, quieter. She wound her way down the steps in search of one of the yacht's many bathrooms. As she wandered the narrow hallways, she realized this yacht was more of a cruise ship, and that this cruise ship was way nicer than any house she'd ever been in.

The espresso hardwood floors shone beneath her feet. Doors opened on room after room, each boasting an enormous bed wrapped in a crisp duvet, the windows offering a killer view of the dark water and clear night sky. At the center of the ship there was a lounge, all supple leather couches and enormous chaise lounges. The Gregorys didn't have to keep up with anyone. Everyone was trying to keep up with them.

When Lina finally came to a door that looked vaguely bathroom-like, she took a chance and pushed it open only to slam directly into one of the most beautiful girls she'd ever seen. Her chocolate skin glowed in the dim lights and her eyes matched the tiny waves licking the edge of the boat. Lush black hair hung down her back and her emerald green dress grazed the middle of her lean, muscled thighs. Lina was pretty sure the girl worked at the Club. She probably made a killing in tips every night.

"Oh, shit, I'm sorry. I didn't even knock." Lina crossed her arms in an attempt to hide the tattoos that lined them. She wanted to disappear and be noticed all at the same time.

She settled for hunching forward and letting the longest strand of her white hair hide her eyes, as if that might make her look like less of a giant, awkward loser who had just barreled into a bathroom like some kind of cretin.

"Lina Winthrop?" The girl grabbed her hand and squeezed gently. "I've been meaning to introduce myself." All of the warmth that Lina had been hoping for in her random kiss upstairs poured into her stomach and flowed down her legs at the touch of the girl's hand.

This is what it's supposed to feel like.

She imagined the girl leaning closer, giving into everything she'd been trying to fight for the last eight years of her life. The girl's lips would graze her own, gentle and light like a butterfly, and she'd tug Lina closer.

"It is Lina, right?" The girl pulled her eyebrows together in confusion and Lina shook her head.

"No, um, I mean yes. Yes, I'm Lina. And you are?" She sounded ruder than she meant to.

"Mari. I've seen you at the Club. I'm a server. Is everything all right? You look lost." Lina hadn't realized that Mari still held her hand. She squeezed gently and then leaned in close, her breath tickled Lina's neck. "Bet I can help." Blood rushed to Lina's cheeks, and it felt like her entire body was blushing. And then, so fast she couldn't be sure if she'd just imagined it, she felt Mari's lips on her ear. "You look like you could use a drink." The girl giggled and handed Lina her glass.

Lina didn't think, she just tipped her head back and let the cool liquid slide down her throat. The drink burned its way down into her stomach, and she involuntarily squeezed her eyes shut as the alcohol coursed through her body. When she opened them, Mari's lips were just a breath away from her own, and more than she had ever wanted anything in her life, Lina wanted to close the space.

But this wasn't how Lina had envisioned her night going. This wasn't who she envisioned spending her night with. This wasn't who Lina was supposed to be.

"I'm . . . good, thanks. I've gotta go." Lina turned and rushed back up the stairs not caring what she looked like. She just had to get out of there. She had to stick with her original plan.

And like a sign from a God she never really believed in, the phone she'd been handed when she boarded the ship buzzed in her clutch.

Mariner's Cove. Now.

She was being summoned by her mystery date. Lina knew this was it. Tonight was the night she'd finally let go of everything and forget all of the other weird shit. She was just a normal girl who didn't really enjoy guys. Sexuality existed on a spectrum like anything else, and she happened to fall in the place where it didn't feel all that good. Maybe if she finally got it over with, maybe then she'd feel differently. Surely instinct would take over. Or something. As Lina made her way through the winding hallways, the boat began to tip and sway. Her head swam. She couldn't quite find her footing. How strange. She must have drunk more than she realized.

When she finally found the room, she was happy to see the bed. She collapsed into its white expanse without even remembering what she was there to do.

Until she saw Trip Gregory.

"You made it."

Her mouth tried to form some type of response but her lips refused to move the right way.

"*This is going to be fun. Promise.*" *Trip smiled, the whites of his teeth blending together into a solid strip, his eyes spreading out and then in.*

Lina began to fade. "My friends . . . I . . . um, I'm supposed to find them." The words slipped out of her mouth. She needed an escape. Something about Trip in the tiny room unsettled her.

"They're fine. Willa's with James. It's just you and me."

Those were the last words she remembered him saying before she blacked out completely.

Later, when her eyes fluttered open, Lina was alone. She heard the fireworks exploding outside the window. Her heavy eyelids only allowed her to see the briefest flashes of red, white, and blue. She wished she were on deck so she could really see them. There was something cozy about fireworks, the way they warmed the night sky, their burnt campfire smell. But tonight she was so tired. It was impossible to keep her eyes open, like there was someone scrubbing her corneas with tiny brillo pads. Sleep seemed to drown her, and this time when the darkness swallowed her up, she was too tired to try to claw her way out.

Minutes or hours or days later Lina opened her eyes and came to a few realizations rather quickly. The first was that she was fully dressed. The second was that the bed was wet. The third was that she wasn't alone.

She remembered the fireworks, her dry mouth, and heavy eyes. And then Trip. What the hell had he done to her?

But when Lina rolled over to examine the snoring boy passed out next to her, Trip was nowhere to be found.

Instead, Lina was sleeping next to a very soaked, very unconscious James Gregory.

And that's when she heard the sirens.

PART 3

A.W.O.L. (Absence With Out Leave)

Chapter 17

Back to the drawing board. 9 2morrow. Same place.

Sloane read Madge's text over and over again, the words swimming in front of her eyes. She wondered what a drawing board looked like. Obviously, she knew that Madge was referring to a theoretical drawing board and not an actual, physical board, but the question sort of got stuck in her brain. Like when one of her uncle's old school records got a scratch and kept playing the same snippet of a song over and over again. Sloane's brain was like that. Sometimes it just got stuck.

And her stupid, scratched, stuck brain couldn't stop imagining a drawing board for the War. Would there be pictures of the Gregorys with bull's eyes printed over their faces? Or maybe pictures of Willa. Her school picture, the snapshot of her and Sloane in Aruba, the sun glinting off Willa's blonde hair. Or maybe even a picture of her when they pulled her out of the lake that night. Sloane hadn't wanted to look, hadn't wanted to see, but she was there when they fished her friend from the dark water. She *remembered*.

Willa's body, bloated and blue from her time under the surface, was another mental sink hole. Sloane dug her fingernails into her palms, worked to switch the image, tried to conjure up Aruba, white sand, Willa's crooked smile, and the sparkling water—but no matter what, she was only ever able to see death. The scratched record in her head played on. As she walked toward the secret entrance to the Club's attic she thought about songs and how supposedly soldiers used horrible pop songs to torture terrorists in remote island prisons. Sloane imagined playing a manufactured pop song over and over again for the Gregorys, while at the same time forcing them to see the image of Willa, still and cold. That was a revenge she could wrap her head around.

Sloane knew the girls' original plan was doomed. The doubt had already taken root and grown like a thorny vine, tightening around her so that the key she wore every day felt more like a noose than anything else. These were Gregorys. They couldn't be damaged by naked pictures and drugs. Nothing could end their reign at Hawthorne. But she never quite found the right moment to tell the girls. Or really, to tell Madge. She saw the determination in her eyes, knew what happened when she set out to win. And she was scared for her. But more than anything, she wished Madge would grieve for Willa like a normal person. The truth was Sloane didn't really understand how destroying the Gregorys was supposed to make them feel any better about losing Willa. In fact, so far, this whole revenge scenario had only made Sloane feel worse.

But in the end, it didn't matter what she thought or felt. This was the central reality of her life: Sloane knew she was dumb. She said dumb things all the time, did dumb things.

She'd learned to compensate for being an idiot by shutting up and agreeing with whatever everyone else said or did.

Getting by was so much easier that way.

Sloane made her way up the stairs, counting them one by one in her head as she ascended, a childhood habit that she could never quite kick thanks to parents who attempted to make every second of her life a teachable moment of some sort. Her earliest memory was of the time her mother forced her to read *Corduroy* out loud at one of the many social gatherings her parents hosted. Each memorized word slipped from between her lips, her voice loud and strong. She knew enough to change her inflection on certain words and to read slowly as though she were truly sounding out the words for the first time, decoding the secret message. But it was a good thing she knew the book by heart because as she "read," the story distracted her. The little girl, Lisa, claimed she loved Corduroy just the way he was as she fixed the strap of his broken overall. But Sloane didn't buy it. Lisa didn't want to make Corduroy more comfortable; she wanted him to look good. Lisa was embarrassed by her beat-down bear in the same way her parents were embarrassed by their dumbass daughter. Even as a little girl she noticed her father flinch when she stumbled over a word. Her parents wanted to parade her around like some kind of trophy they had received for being geniuses. But those genius genes hadn't been passed on. She knew it. They knew it.

And Willa knew it, too.

Sloane had been running late, as usual, when she'd walked into her room to find Willa staring at her PSAT scores that she'd accidentally left out on her desk. Yet another dumb mistake.

"I thought you were a National Merit scholar?" There was

a trace of fear in her voice, the same slight quiver she heard in her parents when she said something outrageously stupid.

If Lina had seen her test results, she would have pretended that it never happened. But Willa was never one to pretend. She always spoke her mind. She always asked really annoying questions. It was one of the things that Sloane hated the most about her dying. All of these people, they remembered Obituary Willa. The real Willa was more than an angel. She was the one who'd busted Sloane for lying about her PSAT scores and called her on it—to help. The one who stayed Sloane's best friend even after she knew Sloane was a fraud. The one who helped Sloane keep her secret.

Muffled voices drifted from beneath the attic door. She hoped she was just late enough. Not so late that she made people worried or annoyed, but the kind of late where you rushed in seemingly frenzied, and the project or the lab—or, in this case, the doomed plan—was already underway: responsibilities assigned, leaders established. For Sloane, running behind was a lifestyle. It cemented her role as a follower, and being a follower minimized her chances of looking like a jackass. If anything in her life came close to an art, it was tardiness.

With a deep breath, she turned the aged bronze handle. "Sorry I'm late, guys." One by one, she examined their faces. Lina's dark eyes softened ever so slightly. Not annoyed. Rose, whom Sloane still couldn't get a read on, smiled when she saw her. Not annoyed. Madge smoothed her perfectly straight hair and avoided making eye contact. Semi-annoyed. But then again Madge was pretty much always semi-annoyed. "What'd I miss?"

"We were just discussing these," Madge said, turning toward Sloane. She wore a crisp white T-shirt. Weird. It must have been brand-new because there were still creases along the center and sleeves. She'd never seen Madge in a T-shirt. "They're for sale in the pro shop."

"Why would anyone want to buy a T-shirt?" The only T-shirts in Sloane's drawer came from random 5K races and Round Robin golf tournaments. Rose shot her an *is-this-girl-for-real?* kind of look just as her brain caught up with her mouth, and she realized she was talking out loud. "Wait, I mean, what's on the front? I can't see it."

Madge pulled the shirt taut across her chest, smoothing out what was emblazoned on the front. There was Trip, naked and grinning, the words WHAT HAPPENS AT THE CLUB STAYS AT THE CLUB in block letters.

"All the money from T-shirt sales goes to the children's hospital," Madge grumbled. "Mr. Freaking Packard had one on."

Mr. Packard was at least ninety years old and was one of the original members of Hawthorne Lake. He spent the bulk of his days in the Club gym, hands behind his head doing these awkward and inappropriate-looking hip exercises. Sloane wondered if he even knew what he was buying. She was pretty sure he was legally blind. He also seemed like the kind of guy who would buy a T-shirt just to buy a T-shirt, so she wasn't sure the fact that he was wearing one proved anything. Either way she really didn't know what to say. Their plan had obviously backfired, and she wasn't sure where that left the girls. She wondered if maybe they should admit defeat and move on like everyone else.

"We're trying to think of our next move," Rose said as Sloane plopped down next to her.

So much for moving on. Sloane wanted to like Rose. Whenever she'd see her around the Club in past summers,

Rose would have her nose stuck in a book—walking and reading, camped out under a tree and reading, sipping a drink and reading. Sloane avoided girls like her because they almost always asked her questions about her favorite book or wanted to know details about her AP classes in school. They made immediate assumptions about her purely based on appearance, and it drove her insane.

But maybe she'd been wrong about Rose. Like Willa, she seemed smart, but not judgy smart. There was a big difference between the two. Still, as much as she wanted to accept Rose, she couldn't. Not completely. Not when Lina's scorn for the girl had suddenly transformed into a twisted sort of friendship.

Sloane's eye caught on Madge's knee, shaking compulsively. Her eyes fixed in space, lost in whatever plan she was trying to develop. Her mouth moved from side to side, lips closed around a mint. She always sucked them these days, and Sloane wondered if maybe she should pick up a habit of her own. Sucking mints seemed to help Madge develop plans. Maybe chewing gum would help Sloane sound smart.

Just as she was about to ask if anyone had a piece of gum, Madge smoothed her dress and stood.

"We have to take a step back." Most people would give up after a failure like the gala but not Madge. It only made her more determined to win. That was the difference between people like Sloane and people like Madge. Sloane would definitely have given up; in fact, she never would have tried in the first place. "We need to strike at the peer level. Hit them where it hurts."

"In the balls?" They were the first words in Sloane's head, and they just sort of flew out of her mouth. It was like she'd taken truth serum or something. God, she wished she had a piece of gum.

But Madge laughed. "Exactly." She let the smile linger on her lips for a beat but then got that faraway look again concentration twisting her features as though she were cramming for the exam of her life. The intensity worried Sloane. She wanted to say that out loud but had no idea how to tell her friend that yes, they needed to take a step back, but without stepping back in again.

"Maybe the Captain is secretly pissed about the pictures. I mean, we don't know for sure it didn't work," Sloane offered meekly. Of course, it was the wrong thing to say.

"I think it's pretty clear where we stand," Madge said to nobody in particular.

"The pictures actually helped them," Lina murmured. She'd been so quiet since the gala, and Sloane knew her friend was hurting so much more than she ever let on. She'd seen the new tattoos carved into the thin skin along Lina's inner wrists like scars. She wished there was something she could do. "We need something better, something that will force the Captain to cut their sorry asses off for good."

Sloane considered Lina's suggestion. If she could just come up with a way to embarrass the Gregorys maybe then her friends would come back. But how *could* you destroy the most popular boys at Hawthorne Lake?

"We could spread rumors," Rose suggested.

The group sat silent. A non-starter.

"How about . . ." Sloane and Lina began at the same time. Sloane's mouth clamped shut.

Lina shook her head. "Oh sorry, Sloaney, you go first."

"Boobs." Sloane said the first thing that came to her mind and regretted it immediately. It was as though the air had been sucked from the already stuffy attic. Madge's eyes narrowed, and she was up in a flash, her body bent in half over Sloane.

"Do you think this is a joke?" Madge asked, breathing heavily.

"No . . . I . . . um . . . Jack what's-his-face . . ." Sloane stammered.

Lina jumped up from her seat in a tattered velvet chair. "Madge, back off!" She started smiling. "Jake Horvatz. Right? Jake Horvatz and his man boobs!"

Sloane couldn't remember a time when Lina had been so excited, and she wished she could jump up and get excited with her friend. Lina got it. She took Sloane's ridiculous "boobs" and translated. She wanted to kiss her.

"Hormone therapy, am I right?" Lina said. She started pacing back and forth in front of Madge. "I have no idea if it would even work, Sloane?" Lina raised her eyebrows at Sloane as though she'd be in some position to weigh in on the topic of hormone therapy and whether or not it might make teenage dudes grow boobs just because her parents were successful doctors. Um . . . no.

"I could ask?" Sloane said, sounding like she needed permission.

Rose shrugged her shoulders. "I can pay off the busboys to slip something in their morning drinks."

"Well, as long as we have enough money left to cover all of this." Madge shot Rose and Lina a meaningful look that Sloane didn't even attempt to interpret.

"We have plenty of money, and oh my God, if they even come close to good old Jake's tatas, it will be a huge success." Lina smiled wickedly. "They can wear Trip's new T-shirts in the pool."

Madge cocked her head. "It's not bad, and it's not like we have a lot of options left given our recent expenditures."

Sloane wasn't entirely sure how boobs would get the boys

disinherited. She was only sure she was missing something. (Maybe it was a two-stage plan?) Actually, that wasn't true. Sloane was sure of something else: Willa would have loved this. One time she'd sent them all personal letters from the Captain informing them of a new dress code at the Club that required single young women to wear ankle-length skirts at all times on the Club premises. She, Madge, and Lina actually showed up looking like Amish girls before they figured out that Willa had forged the letter. And then before she could stop it from happening, Sloane saw Willa's ghostlike body on the sand. If it weren't for her eyes, open and unseeing, she might have been sleeping, dreaming about her last year of high school before college.

Her eyes, her eyes, her eyes.

Sloane's brain stuck on the image for a moment. She knew from experience that the more she tried to make it go away, the more clear the image became, that the sooner she let it consume her, the sooner it'd be over.

"I think it's a great idea," she said blankly.

Maybe if she went along with the plan, Willa wouldn't have to haunt her anymore. Maybe she'd be able to forget how her friend's beautifully clear blue eyes had turned solid white. How they seemed to scream silently into the blackness. Willa's eyes told Sloane that she had fought until the final moment.

Her eyes, her eyes, her eyes . . .

Maybe the record scratch wasn't a bad thing this time. It reminded Sloane that she owed it to her friend to fight the same way now.

Chapter 18

Sloane arrived even later than usual to the hospital in hopes that her parents would eat without her or at least discuss her academic standing before she got there. She could never be late enough. There they were. Waiting. At the same table with the same disgusting hospital food that smelled like disinfectant mixed with canned vegetables. Of course, she had gotten used to the smell of hospitals a long time ago. After all, she had practically grown up in their antiseptic halls. Sloane's parents were OBGYNs who specialized in high-risk pregnancies. Women came from all over the world, reeking of hope, to be treated by her world-famous parents.

When she was little, her nanny brought her and her little sister to the hospital every single night so they could eat dinner as a family. Except for Sundays. On Sundays, the Lius ate at home. Mail was cleared off the kitchen table, place settings arranged, and dinner cobbled together by Sloane and her mom. But after a while it got kind of annoying to have someone interrupt every five seconds with a page or a phone call, so Sunday dinners were transferred to the hospital like every-thing else. Family time on doctor's terms. Her parents loved having their hospital Jell-O and eating it, too.

"Hi, honey, was traffic awful?" Sloane's mother asked, hopping up to squeeze her in a tight hug. Her mother always blamed her lateness on traffic even though traffic was pretty much non-existent. She just couldn't process Sloane acting like anything less than the perfect daughter. And perfect daughters were on time.

When Sloane was accused of cheating on a Spanish test, they insisted that her private school pay for the teacher's eyes to be tested. Turns out she was nearsighted. A week later she was unemployed.

When Sloane missed curfew because she passed out behind the boathouse at the Club's Summer Swing, they were sure Sloane must have narcolepsy. She didn't, but that hadn't stopped her parents from putting her on some crazy drug. Not Xanax, but some scary sounding X-name. Willa was the one (of course) who finally convinced Sloane that they were making her a zombie. Too scared to admit to her parents that she'd quit taking them, she'd started secretly giving them away to some busboy at the Club—a kid named Rory who claimed he needed them for his sister. It was like charity. Or something.

But when Sloane ended up with a 900 on her SATs, her parents were at a loss. Sure, they discussed the test being biased against minorities, a hot-button topic in the Liu house-hold. But she was freaking Chinese. Asian kids always aced standardized testing. For a while they went with the whole, "the test doesn't really measure your intelligence" approach and did a bunch of IQ testing—but they never showed Sloane the results and quickly changed tactics. Presumably she'd managed to pull in a score roughly equivalent to her dress size. After running out of excuses, her parents were left with no choice but to take action and hire a tutor.

"So, Sloaney, how's test prep going? Dr. Yang's son swears he never would have gotten into Yale without his private tutor."

Sloane stabbed some wilted salad with her fork and pretended it was Jude Yang's face. He was such an arrogant little bastard. She needed to piece together some type of intelligent response, but the truth raced through her head, another broken record.

Test prep sucks because I'm dumb. Test prep sucks because I'm dumb. Test prep sucks because I'm dumb.

You're wasting your money; I want to give up. You're wasting your money; I want to give up. You're wasting your money; I want to give up.

I am not the daughter you really wanted. I am not the daughter you really wanted. I am not the daughter you really wanted . . .

"Sloane?" Her dad's brow furrowed. For a second Sloane worried that her thoughts had somehow dodged her filter and exploded out of her mouth again.

"Is Dr. Harvey not doing a good job?" her mother chimed in. "Because if you find he's moving too slow for you, I'm sure we can get a new tutor, someone with more credentials? Honestly, we probably should have done it from day one, don't you think, honey?" She looked at Sloane's father expectantly and he nodded.

"Absolutely, absolutely. Whatever it takes to get Sloane a score that won't reflect poorly on her stellar academic record."

Right. The stellar academic record that she'd managed to maintain by cheating. At this point in the conversation, it occurred to Sloane that she hadn't said a single word since she arrived at the hospital. As usual her parents spoke over her and around her. Always assuming the best, never acknowledging the worst.

"So, I have a question." Sloane blurted out the words before she lost her courage.

Her mother dropped her spoon on the table. Her father choked on a hunk of bread. Shock was a good sign. She'd be more likely to get an honest answer. She barreled onward. "What kind of hormones would give a guy . . . boobs?" A fierce blush swept across her cheeks. When you spoke as little as Sloane did, saying the word "boobs" out loud was kind of mortifying—especially in front your parents. She'd said the word *twice* today.

"Is this the kind of subject Dr. Harvey is having you study? If so, I think it is highly inappropriate." Her mother's delicate features twisted into a scowl.

"No, Mom, it's not that. I'm just . . . curious."

Her mother's eyes flashed to her father. They must have come to some unspoken agreement that he should take it from there.

"Well, it's certainly possible for men to develop breasts, but it takes a lot of time and a lot of drugs with a variety of side effects."

"Like what?"

"Loss of sexual arousal is common."

Sloane's parents were the type who took pride in always answering their daughter honestly. Too bad they were so good at lying to themselves.

"Like how long?"

"Months, sometimes years. Why do you ask, Sloaney? Is everything okay? This isn't like you." Her father's voice was heavy with concern. Sloane was struck how the very act of asking a question sent her parents completely off balance. She was so passive, so good at pretending to be the perfect Stepford Asian daughter that they had no idea how to react when she was her real self. And to add insult to injury or as Sloane said, injury to insult, the War couldn't afford years or even months. The disappointment must have shown on her face.

"Honey, if you are confused about your sexuality, you can talk to us." Her mother looked so earnest, Sloane couldn't bear to look at her. She was trying so hard to do the right thing. And failing. Miserably.

"It's natural for a girl of your age to want to look a certain way, but you are so proportional, so beautiful the way you are. Did Lina put this idea into your head?" As usual her father was trying to deflect blame, to do whatever it took to keep his perfect daughter perfect. Even if she only existed in his eyes.

Sloane thought about telling them the truth. Her parents hadn't been at the Club when Willa was killed and had only rushed to the beach after the fact. They were so busy with work and so focused on Sloane that they were completely oblivious to the rumors that swirled around about the Gregorys. Maybe if she told them the truth, they'd help her do something to fix this mess.

"Oh honey, we're so proud of you and your choices. You're smart and beautiful and you're going to ace the SATs this fall. I just know it."

"We're always here for you, Sloane. Just keep making us proud. Okay, honey?" Her dad tugged on her ponytail fondly and smiled broadly at her mother.

So. That conversation was over before it even started. Probably all for the best.

Even though it hurt her cheeks to do it, Sloane smiled back.

Chapter 19

Sloane gazed out the attic window at what looked like a monsoon. Rain pounded onto the rooftop, each drop exploding like a mini bomb. Valets scurried around in dripping raincoats emblazoned with Hawthorne Lake's monogram. Members ducked under the portico, dry and comfortable as they waited for their needs to be met. In the attic, her friends' voices droned, blending in with the steady, violent patter. As much as she knew she should be listening, a loyal soldier in the War hanging on every word, she couldn't bring herself to tune in.

Instead, she squinted toward the beach, the water grey and ominous. If Willa were alive, she might have been down there alone, letting the rain pelt her back as she bent to pick up the smooth pieces of glass the lake spit out. She used to say they were easiest to find in the rain, the drops washing away sand that normally hid the tiny treasures. She'd always give the prettiest piece to Sloane. The smooth glass nestled into the palm of Sloane's hand would feel warm and smooth. That feeling would snake its way up through her arm all through her body. Like magic. That's what it was like being friends with Willa. Magic. But there was no one on the beach now. And with no magic glass to warm her palm, a sickening emptiness wormed its way into her heart instead.

"You heard Sloane," Madge said. "Her parents said it would take months. We don't have months. We barely have weeks. Summer's almost over."

Sloane perked up when she heard her name. She'd already discussed the boob failure ad nauseum. It wasn't going to work, just like everything else. She turned from the window.

"I like the idea of spiking their drinks," Rose said, twirling a strand of hair around her finger. "I know so many servers who'd want in. What if we used laxatives instead of hormones?"

Lina sat up straighter, raising her eyebrows. "The golf tournament is at the beginning of the month. We can have all the bathrooms locked. They'll shit their pants. Literally."

The girls thought on this for a moment. Sloane pictured Trip running around with his hand cupping his butt. Man boobs and shitting your pants—it was all the same, wasn't it? Enough to embarrass, but not enough to destroy. She was grateful that Madge shook her head.

"We have almost thirty-five thousand dollars left, and all we can come up with is a colon cleanse? We're better than this." Madge began pacing the small attic.

Sloane turned back to the window, watching the drops slide down the glass like worms.

"You could steal Viagra from the hospital, Sloaney," Lina piped up. "Rose, you arrange for it to be slipped into drinks at the Mother-Son banquet and the boys have to walk around with unsightly lumps in their pants like sex offenders. It'll be epic. Especially around a bunch of moms."

More of the same, Sloane thought. She imagined the boys bantering about sexy cougar-moms and could practically hear MILF jokes and the laughter that followed. They'd twist it around to their advantage, as usual. They should have learned from the fundraiser that the Gregorys were master manipulators. But she didn't know how to voice any of it.

As if on cue her gaze was drawn to a shock of red hair under the portico. Trip Gregory stood there, stretching to look at the sky, probably considering making a dash for it. He spoke with the valet for a moment, his face warm and inviting, the typical grin stretched along his jaw line. But when the valet ducked back inside, Trip's eyes narrowed into slits and a grimace replaced his usual smile. A crystal glass from the bar was gripped between his fingers and his gaze zeroed in on the tiny window of the attic.

Oh my God.

He saw her. She was sure of it. And before she could duck out of sight, he cocked his head and released his fingers from the tumbler. The glass fell as though in slow motion, exploding around his feet and mirroring the jagged smile that flashed over his face. Sloane threw herself on the attic floor. For some reason, she was reminded of spinning with her friends when she was a little girl, tiny hands clasped together singing, *"Ashes, ashes we all fall . . . DOWN!"* They'd giggle hysterically as they fell. This time no one was laughing.

"Sloane, what the hell? Are you okay?" Lina tried to help her up, but Sloane yanked her down. "Ouch! Let go of my arm. What's your problem?" She shook Sloane off of her and struggled to her feet.

"Trip! He saw me. He dropped a glass and it broke and he smiled. You guys, I think he knows." Sloane rose on her knees and peered out the window, careful to remain partially hidden. She kept her eyes trained on the ground outside the Club, certain if she tried hard enough she'd be able to make out the shards of glass. The valet pulled up in Trip's black BMW, and Sloane watched as he walked toward the car. His affable smile was back in place. Before he opened the door, he stood in the rain and lifted his arm in a mocking salute directed at Sloane. Funny, even in her terror, all she could think was, *He doesn't even care about soaking that expensive watch. He doesn't care about anything . . .*

And that's when it hit her.

It didn't happen often and she could never be sure when it was coming, but she was sometimes struck out of the blue with an idea. The last one had been "boobs," of course. This one was much better.

"Watches," Sloane blurted as she turned from the window to the group.

Back in the day, when Great Grandpa Gregory and his brother began making real money, they'd bought a pair of valuable watches, gifts to each other for hard work and sacrifice. Now James and Trip had inherited them. Instead of representing hard work and sacrifice, they stood for wealth and the life of leisure that came with other people working hard for you. There had to be a way to use the watches against them. They were family heirlooms. They could drive a wedge between Grandpa and the twins, couldn't they?

The girls frowned. Madge opened her mouth, but before she could say a word, footsteps pounded up the stairwell. All of the girls jumped out of their seats and rushed together to defend themselves against whoever had come to destroy everything. Sloane's heart exploded in her chest. It was Trip. It had to be.

But when the door flew open, she saw two housekeepers.

Sloane blinked at them. Had Trip sent them? They shut the door and faced the girls in the standard navy blue house-keeping uniforms, an H and L stitched at their breast. They looked like twins, with their dull, almost greyish-blonde hair secured at the nape of their necks with bobby pins. They couldn't have been much older than the girls. Rose rushed forward.

"Kira, Nadia, what's wrong?"

"We didn't want to be late." The older one spoke in a slight Russian accent. "We want to join. For Pavla."

Madge glared at Rose.

"I didn't tell anyone, I swear." Rose raised her hands, her dark eyes large and insistent.

"No one invited us. The Gregory boys. We heard them talking. They know you are behind the pictures. Lina, she took the picture of Trip, yes?"

Lina nodded, her lips pursed.

"You must be careful. We will help you." The younger one spoke this time, her eyes focused steadily on the floor, hands wringing.

"How could you have heard all of this?" Madge demanded. "You mean to tell me that Trip and James were just openly discussing this at the Club?"

"They talk in the library. We were cleaning." The older one sounded defensive, and Rose must have picked up on her tone.

"They're maids. Of course they speak freely around them. They probably don't even realize they speak English." Rose sounded angry, frustrated. For the first time it occurred to Sloane that Rose had probably been ignored at one time or another as well.

"Who's Pavla?" Lina asked.

"Our sister. The Captain accused Pavla of stealing his

wife's necklace during a massage but she would never steal. The Captain lied because she refused to . . ." The girl let her voice trail off, embarrassed and ashamed of what the Captain had asked of her sister.

"She was fired. And now she's back in Russia." The other sister finished.

It was no drowning in Hawthorne Lake, but it was something bad, evil, and twisted. Sloane wondered how many other people at the Club had their own Willas.

"Let them in," Sloane heard herself say.

Rose nodded. "They could help with the inside stuff. They have access. They can keep track of what the boys are planning."

The younger one finally lifted her head and offered a sad, tentative smile.

Madge and Lina looked at each other, and Lina lifted her bony shoulders. "We need them," she said, and then caught herself, "I mean, we need you. But this is War, so get ready for the long haul." She lowered herself back into the couch, flustered.

"There might be no war to fight if we can't think of a new idea," Madge snapped. She popped her last mint in her mouth. Bad sign. She had to be nearing the end of her reserves, and they'd gotten practically nowhere. Rain continued to pound on the roof. The young maids hesitated at the door, but finally came forward and sat on the floor, tucking their legs beneath them.

Sloane retreated into her head once again. Watches. Pavla. Stolen necklace. Antiques. Valuable jewelry. They could make fun of the watches. They could destroy the watches. They could hide the watches. They could steal the watches. She sat up straighter. They *could* steal the watches.

"We steal the watches!" Sloane practically shouted the words.

All eyes flicked to her. She got that panicky feeling that accompanied the pressure of the spotlight. Like she was "reading" *Corduroy* all over again. Her pulse raced as she considered, shaking her head, shutting up. Then she remembered the casual way Trip had smashed the glass in front of the Club. How a Gregory didn't care who he hurt or what he broke; he just liked the sound of something shattering. And that's when she realized: it didn't matter if they lost. The War *had* to be fought. Maybe they didn't stand a chance against the Gregorys. But Sloane was going to go down fighting, like Willa.

Besides, no one knew she was dumb here. Not like Willa knew. They might have suspected it, but it wasn't like at school. The girls here didn't know about how she cheated her way to her As, they didn't whisper how two of the most intelligent doctors in the country had raised such a complete idiot. It might not be the answer to the War, but at least it was a start.

"Get it?" Sloane asked, knowing this could go only one of two ways.

"You. Are. A. Genius." Four words from Madge. Four simple words and Sloane's heart soared. "Great Grandpa Gregory and their great uncle passed down those watches. They're antiques. Priceless. Oh my God, Sloane. That's it!"

Sloane felt her confidence grow as Lina beamed at her, and Rose gave her thumbs up, which felt so, so good in spite of its inherent dorkiness. Even the Russian sisters nodded enthusiastically. "We could sell them. Make it look like they needed gambling money or whatever. That would really piss off Gramps."

"ON EBAY!" Lina shouted. "We sell them on eBay." She laughed maniacally, and everyone couldn't help but join in. Sloane laughed the loudest for once. Turns out being a dumbass had its moments.

Chapter 20

It was the first time Sloane had seen James Gregory sober since Willa died. His aviators hid most of his face. Judging from the greenish tint of his complexion, she guessed he was recovering from yet another bender. But it was Sunday morning and that meant golf with the Captain. And lucky for the girls, his fancy watch got in the way of his golf swing. It was the only time he ever took it off.

Sloane watched him warm up at the driving range from a bench partially hidden by trees. She had a magazine as an alibi should it come to that. She was staring, after all. She had no idea what the perfect golf swing was supposed to look like, but her guess was that James had to be pretty close. Or maybe she was just making assumptions based on his perfect body.

Somehow she had landed the job of monitoring James while Rose stole the set of master keys from her mom's desk and slipped them to Kira and Nadia. Lina and Madge were supposed to be watching Trip at the basketball courts. If either Gregory made a move toward the Club lockers, the girls were supposed to text a warning to everyone. God bless technology.

James took a break from his practice and used his driver to stretch his shoulders, his pink golf shirt creeping up and revealing a sliver of toned, tanned stomach. Sloane couldn't stop herself from leaning forward on the bench to get a better look.

"If you're waiting for me to pass out midswing, it's not gonna happen," he called.

At first Sloane figured he had to be talking to someone else. He hadn't even bothered turning to look at her. She grabbed her magazine and pretended to read just to be safe.

"That's upside down, you know."

He laughed hoarsely. His voice was louder. Footsteps approached. She looked up and found James standing directly in front of her. Close enough that she could smell last night's drinks on his skin and see this morning's stubble along his jaw.

She opened her mouth to say something, wrapped her lips around imagined words, but no sound came out. She thought about running. It would be safest to run. There was no telling what James might do to her. She should have thought of that before she agreed to do this alone, but none of the other girls were taking the Gregorys seriously yet. And now Sloane was on the golf course, blatantly spying on James. Calling their bluff.

Her movements were calculated and slow. *Don't make eye contact*, she thought. As if maybe if she didn't look at him he wouldn't be able to see her. Sloane looked up through her eyelashes. Yup. Still there. *Shit. Shit. Shit. What the hell am I supposed to do now?*

"Can I ask you something." It wasn't a question. Gregorys almost never asked questions.

She nodded. Her head was light with adrenaline and fear. He was going to ask her about the pictures. Accuse her of plotting against them. He was going to threaten to kill her just the way he'd killed Willa.

"What do you remember about that night?" His voice was cold.

He couldn't be serious. Was this some kind of test? A joke? Maybe the girls had already been caught, and he was just toying with her before the Captain swooped in and exiled her to some SAT prep summer camp.

"Uh, you mean . . ." Sloane stammered, hoping to buy herself some time.

"Yeah, that night. The Fourth of July. What the hell night do you think I mean?" James ran his shaky fingers through his thick blond hair. "I don't remember anything. I . . . just need to know, I need to know what I did to her." His voice cracked on the last word.

It was a trick. It had to be a trick. He was baiting her. Trying to get her to expose her friends. He had to be because there was no way he didn't remember that night. How the hell could he kill someone and not remember anything about it? But when she looked up at him, she saw nothing threatening. In fact, he almost looked hopeful. Not to mention scared. Like she, Sloane, might be able to help him figure this whole mess out. He kind of looked like someone might look if they really didn't remember killing a person.

It was his eyes. They were bleary, yet somehow serious. Focused behind the alcohol and pain. She remembered watching Willa look up into his eyes that night. Jealous of how she laughed as she navigated the party. Jealous of her ease, of the way she moved, talked, and existed without even having to think about it. Sloane hung on her every word, wondering if she tried hard enough, if she could fake it. Like *Corduroy*. And when Willa left and wasn't around to watch, she moved onto Lina, Madge, and other girls at the Club. While her friend fought for her life, she was fighting to fit in.

"I remember . . ." Just as Sloane began, a sharp voice cut her off.

"James!" The Captain stood on the green, his wiry grey hair perfectly combed, his golf shirt with Hawthorne Lake's monogram crisp. It was already close to eighty degrees, but his face didn't flush, his shirt wasn't damp. Apparently it took more than moderate global warming to make the Captain sweat.

"Just do me one favor. Tell Rose I don't remember, okay?" James's blue eyes pierced into Sloane. He was practically begging. Gregorys never begged. "I've seen you with her. I know you guys talk. Just . . . just tell her."

Sloane nodded in silent shock, too confused to do anything but agree with whatever he was asking of her. Her phone vibrated on the bench next to her. It was a text from Madge.

GOT THEM

A picture of two gold watches popped up on the screen.

Sloane should have felt excited. She should have been celebrating. The girls were on their way. But sitting on that bench, staring at those watches as James Gregory and his grandfather climbed into a golf cart, the only thing Sloane felt was terror. Terror that one of her best friends was dead, and she had actually spoken to the guy who had killed her. Terror that all of her friends were working so hard to destroy him. Terror because when James said he didn't remember, she believed him.

She needed a minute, an hour, a day to try to process what was going on. But she was smart enough to know that time was the one thing she didn't have. The watches were already ticking.

Chapter 21

The rest of the hot day passed in a blur. Madge's paranoia upon learning that the Gregorys were onto them had compelled her to set up an unnecessarily complex hand-off process (in Sloane's opinion, anyway)—one that involved Sloane fishing the watches out of a garbage can in the ladies locker room.

Now she was home alone with the watches, obsessing over their brand-spanking-new eBay listing. The ceiling fan above her head spun and rattled like it was on decapitation setting, seconds away from flying down and chopping her to pieces. Although maybe that would be a good thing. Maybe if the stupid fan fell down, it would dice up her guilt, along with the rest of her, into such small pieces that no one would ever know it'd been there in the first place. Maybe the fan's blades would open her up and reveal her guts, blackened and rotted for not being brave enough to save Willa and for failing her again when she'd spoken to James.

Of course if Sloane died in a freak ceiling fan accident, she wouldn't be able to check the status of their eBay listing.

She rolled over to the opposite side of her bed where her phone lay nestled on a pillow, once again swiping and clicking her way to the post she had created for the "Rare Vintage Cartier Men's Watches." It was fascinating to watch the bids roll in, to wonder if the Captain took the bait after Madge had sent him the listing. It was downright exhilarating to imagine their plan, *Sloane's* plan, working.

CCG1927 outbid a***y AGAIN. Up to $19,876.

She sent the message to the girls despite the fact that they could easily keep track as well. It felt good to be doing something right for once. Then again, she'd practically pulled her hair out over the listing, using a combination of a thesaurus, Wikipedia, and other eBay listings to cobble together what she hoped would be one coherent auction. But she was proud. She'd even learned how to return messages to potential buyers, copying and pasting vintage Cartier facts scored from a Google search. She liked to imagine the bidders—a creepy old man with gnarled fingers hunched over an old desktop computer buying back a watch from his glory days, a desperate housewife determined to win back her husband from his hot new secretary, a devoted mother buying a graduation present for her only son.

But there was one bidder who she didn't have to imagine at all. Sloane was positive that CCG stood for a scrambling Charles Cornelius Gregory. Perhaps he was this much closer to disinheriting his worthless grandsons. Madge had been the one in charge of sending the Captain the link to the listing via a newly set up email address. Sloane could almost feel the satisfaction Madge must have felt when she'd clicked send. The very thought of the Captain having to register for an eBay account was a small victory.

Sloane refreshed the auction again. Another two bids came through neck-and-neck.

James. James. James.

She couldn't stop thinking about him. The auction didn't distract her; it only heightened the obsession. Willa had once told her that James used to black out when he was drinking. They'd have entire conversations that he wouldn't remember the next day. It drove her insane. He'd been sober for the past year, so Sloane had nearly forgotten about James's alcohol-induced memory loss. But now . . . what if James was telling the truth? What if he really didn't remember anything that happened on the Fourth of July? She remembered him swaying on the boat, his eyes bleary and unfocused. Would that make Willa's death a terrible accident or the murder they'd all assumed it was? Did murderers ever forget? The lines she'd always seen so crisply drawn were suddenly turning hazy, wavering along the edges. Destruction of the Gregory boys had only seemed fair when she was sure James had killed her best friend on purpose. Eye for an eye and all that. Now, the spark she'd felt that first day in the attic fizzled out, the smoke leaving a bad taste in her mouth.

But Sloane had to do her part. The War was for Willa, yes, but Madge was still alive and they all deserved to know the truth. Doing her part meant keeping the watches safe and hidden. Their housekeeper had come way too close to uncovering them earlier in the day. She could just imagine Helene reporting to her parents and the after-school-special-esque conversation that would inevitably follow. Her parents would probably think she was planning on selling them to pay for a boob job. In the end, Sloane decided the safest place for the watches was on her body, in a small fanny pack that she had used on her class trip to France to hold her passport and Euros.

James. James. James.

She threw her phone in her bag and hopped out of bed. She needed something to do. Somewhere to go. Her legs were jittery and her brain was stuck on a new track, the one where it kept replaying James's voice.

"I can't remember. I can't remember. I can't remember."

Sloane couldn't stop herself from responding.

I can't forget. I can't forget. I can't forget.

Ice cream. She needed ice cream. Something cold, creamy, and distracting. Ben and Jerry's was a ten-minute walk from her house. It would be good to get out, stretch her legs, and maybe even find a new broken record for her brain.

Sloane slipped into her flip-flops, left a note for Helene, and trotted down her narrow driveway onto the sidewalk. The enormous oak trees that lined her street created a shady canopy for her as she meandered toward the ice cream shop. Sprinklers sprayed her legs as she went, the drops of water sparking in the sun. It felt good to be outside, alone for once. She hadn't realized how much she needed this.

"Sloane?" Someone gasped for breath behind her. "Is that you?"

A red-faced, sweaty Jude Yang ran to catch up. If there was anything she *didn't* need right now, it was Jude Yang. He was wearing a Yale T-shirt with the arms cut off revealing sinewy biceps. Every time Sloane saw him, he was decked out in head-to-toe Yale gear. He was only a freshman. He must have bought every single article of clothing they were selling at the damn school bookstore.

"Oh, hey." Sloane lowered her head, turned, and kept walking, praying that he'd get the hint. She knew she shouldn't hate him. Jude had been valedictorian last year, was an exceptional musician, a star lacrosse player, ridiculously good-looking, and nice. His father worked at the hospital with her parents. He was all they ever talked about. He was everything Sloane wasn't, everything everyone wanted *her* to be. And she hated him for it.

"I just don't see why you don't give him a chance," Willa had once said to Sloane as they lay on the deck of Sloane's parents' boat. "You'd make the perfect couple, and he's always staring at you. Everyone sees it." She'd hoisted herself up on an elbow then, peering over her sunglasses, waiting for Sloane's reaction.

Sloane could have listed a million reasons why she shouldn't give Jude Yang a chance but didn't bother. When Willa got an idea in her head, it was impossible to change it. Willa waited a few more seconds, and when it was clear Sloane wasn't going to respond, she flopped back onto her towel.

"No one's perfect." Willa had practically whispered the words.

Sloane had never been sure exactly who she'd been talking about that day, but the memory had a tendency to pop back up when Jude was around.

"Hey, wait up." Jude trotted next to her.

Sloane angled her body toward the street and kept walking, pretending to be engrossed with her phone.

"I just wanted to say I'm so sorry about . . . about what happened," he offered awkwardly. "I know you two were super tight."

"Oh, um, yeah. It . . . sucks." Tears welled in Sloane's eyes, and she wasn't sure if she was about to cry for Willa or because she sounded so stupid. She had no words and she hated being forced to find some. The last thing she needed was Jude moving in for an awkward hug or something. Her fanny pack felt as if it were squeezing the air out of her body.

She grabbed at the strap, hoping to loosen it, but hit the buckle instead and the bag went flying out from under her shirt. It struck the pavement with a sickening crunch.

Shit. Shit. Shit.

Ninja 101 must have been a required course at Yale because Jude was on the ground grabbing the bag before Sloane could even breathe.

"That didn't sound good." He handed her the bag carefully.

Sloane's hand shook as she pulled the zipper. The watches were broken, they had to be. She was so screwed. So, so, so screwed. She gingerly removed one. Her fingers trembled harder. Sure enough, the glass on the face was cracked.

"Dammit." She swore under her breath, tears pricking her eyes again.

"Oh man, I'm so sorry. Those look important." Jude's voice was so earnest, so kind. Sloane had the sudden urge to knee him in the balls. None of this would have happened if he hadn't stopped her. Goddamned Jude Yang was ruining her freaking life.

"They're like antiques or something, right?" Jude lifted one of the heavy gold watches and ran his finger over the face. If Sloane hadn't been so miserable she would have swatted his hand away. "Cartier. These things have to be worth a fortune. Hey, at least this one isn't broken." He shot her a reassuring smile. "Glass half full, right?"

Sloane could think of a number of places for Jude to stuff his glass.

But then Jude flipped the watch and lines appeared on his forehead. He brought the back closer to his face and narrowed his eyes. "Huh. I'm surprised there's no inscription on the back. My dad's is engraved with the year and product line and stuff."

Uh-oh. Doubt made her breath catch. What if they had stolen the wrong watches? Why did she always feel like she was one step behind? But more than that, why did it feel like it was everyone's goal in life to make her look like a jackass? Including Jude.

He noticed her disappointment. "Oh . . . I'm sure these are just too rare. They probably didn't start engraving the back until the eighties or something."

"Yeah . . . right." She took the watch from Jude and tucked it back into the bag in an effort to excuse herself.

"Hey, I know a guy who could fix the other one for you. It's not too far. I could walk you."

"No." The word slipped out before Sloane could stop herself. "I mean, thanks, but you should finish your run. I think I know the place you're talking about. I'll be fine."

"It's right up on Cedar. If you tell him you know me, he'll give you a deal. Yale man."

Sloane squeezed her eyes shut, then forced them open. If he said the word "Yale" one more time, she would snap. "Awesome. Bye." This time Sloane didn't feel even the tiniest pin prick of remorse when she left Jude Yang standing near the curb. Honestly, she was bolting for his own good.

By the time she made it to the jewelry store, Sloane's cheeks were moist with tears. At least the guy at the counter wasn't emblazoned in Yale. He was just a paunchy middle-aged nerd with a grey beard and glasses. She handed him the watch, desperate for him to say he could fix the complete mess she'd made of the situation. But when the jeweler's eyebrows pulled together in the exact same way that Jude's had as he ran his rough fingers over the back, all remaining hope whooshed out of her. She was defeated. Done. The War was over.

"I don't really see the point in doing anything here," the guy said.

"But it's an antique. It's rare and expensive," Sloane insisted.

"It's antique. Antique junk. It's a fake." The jeweler scrunched his face a little, knowing the truth hurt. "You still want me to fix it?"

What the hell? Sloane couldn't speak past the lump in her throat. She shook her head instead and gathered the watches together, stuffing them back into the fanny pack.

The door jingled as Sloane pulled it open, a notification buzzing on her phone as it slammed behind her.

Another bid. This time only one came in. CCG1927. $30,000.

Fewer than six hours and twenty-three minutes until the auction closed.

It made her brain hurt. Did the Captain know the watches were fake? If he knew, why would he bid the thirty grand? And what about the boys? Would supposedly selling their watches for cash on eBay even be enough to get them cut off? The fact that Sloane didn't have any of the answers made her feel even more dumb than usual. It was like playing rock, paper, scissors. Sloane hated that game because she could never remember what was supposed to beat what so she always ended up playing rock. Rocks were hard. Rocks could smash. Rocks should always win. But the other girls must have figured out her strategy because they always played paper. She hated the feeling of one of their hands enveloping her fist. It wasn't fair. Paper was weak. Paper shouldn't beat anything. Not ever.

And now she couldn't shake the feeling that she had

somehow messed up the rules of the game again. That she'd thrown rock only to have the Captain wrap his wrinkled hand over her fist. Money was made of paper, and money was power. In the rock, paper, scissors game they played at the Club, the Captain always won.

Chapter 22

We did it!

Sloane sat at the ice cream counter, staring at the text. Clearly Madge had seen the $30,000 bid from the Captain. Madge thought they had this locked up, but Sloane knew better. She picked up the cracked watch she'd put on the sticky Formica next to her phone, willing the jagged lines to fuse back together. No dice. At least she was alone—except for the pimply kid behind the counter who had long since retired to the back to do whatever one does with a freezer full of ice cream and far too much time on his hands.

"Who the hell passes down a fake watch?" she whispered.

The bell attached to the door jangled in response.

"I thought that was you." Rose had managed to control that weird habit she had of making everything she said sound like a question. Her long brown hair curled and frizzed in a million different directions but there was no denying she was beautiful—especially today, wearing a strappy sundress instead of her usual cargo shorts.

"Celebrating with a double scoop?" Rose slid onto the stool next to her.

"Not even close."

"A triple then?"

"No, I mean I'm not celebrating." Sloane felt her cheeks flush. "I mean, I think I've messed everything up. Bad." She handed Rose the watch.

Rose held it up to the light and ran her finger over its cracked face. "They can fix this you know. I know it looks bad, but they'll replace the glass, and you won't even know it happened."

"It's not the crack." Sloane took it and slipped it back into her fanny pack.

"Then what?" There was an edge to Rose's voice. Her patience was wearing thin.

She swallowed. "They're fake." It wasn't the whole truth, the important truth. But it was something.

"What do you mean?" Rose's face darkened.

"I mean, they're fake. The watches. Not real."

"But . . . why?" Rose shook her head.

Sloane suddenly had a vision of what she must have looked like at the jewelry store, like a woman who found out her engagement ring was made of paste or a guy who discovered his fiancée was really a dude. "I have no idea." She poked at her ice cream with a plastic spoon. "And it doesn't explain why the Captain would have bid thirty Gs on them this afternoon."

"Unless he didn't know they were fake." Rose sat up a little in her seat. "Maybe the boys already sold them."

"You think?" Sloane's mind was still turning over the idea

in her head, letting it play over and over again until it started to make sense.

"We could always check the police files. I could have sworn I saw something in Trip's about a watch."

Rose stood. Sloane just sat there staring at her ice cream melting, wondering if the truth even mattered anymore. "We'll figure this out, right?" She so badly wanted Rose to tell her that they would fix this together. That they'd make this right for Willa. That there would be justice.

"Yes." Rose placed her hand on Sloane's shoulder. She sounded so confident. So sure. "Sloane, listen to me. We're in this together. Let me help you, okay?"

Half an hour later, they were sitting side-by-side on Rose's bed, flipping through the details of Trip's escapades. Sloane was struck by the strangeness of it all. That not a mile from her house, Rose's stood, cramped and dingy, minutes away, worlds away. She hadn't even known Rose existed before the War, and now she depended on her the way she might have depended on Willa if she were still alive. The understanding made her dizzy.

"There's nothing here about a watch." Rose sighed and tossed the file onto the floor. "I know I saw something though."

Sloane grabbed a thick document from the bottom of the pile, and she forced herself to read the words on the cover: LAST WILL AND TESTAMENT. She needed to focus. "What's that doing in the police files?"

"Dunno. But I'm glad it's here. My dad saves all kinds of crap from his investigations. He must have been holding onto it for reason." Rose paged through the ridiculously long document, and Sloane closed her eyes for a moment.

"Tell her I don't remember."

Goddamn James again. The second she closed her eyes he was there. Taunting her.

"Wait, here's something." Rose's voice momentarily vanquished James from Sloane's brain. *"'To my Grandson Trip, who makes it impossible to forget. Because of this, you have already received your full inheritance from me. Including the Cartier watch handed down from my brother Victor. Don't bother selling it. It's fake. Gotcha.'"*

"I had no idea they could use words like 'gotcha' in a legal document." Sloane couldn't keep the note of wonder out of her voice.

"I might have added that for color," Rose admitted with a laugh.

Sloane's mind raced. "So the Captain knew all along they were fakes. But why bid on them on eBay? Sloane still wasn't making the connection. It didn't quite make sense.

"I think the Captain just likes to mess with people . . . because he can." Rose flopped backward on her double bed with its threadbare flowered duvet and matching ruffle pillows. It looked like the room of a fourth grader, not that Sloane would say that out loud. "Besides, it's not like he can really do anything about it now. He needs them to wear those watches so people don't realize the true extent of his asshole tendencies."

"So, now what?"

"We wait," Rose said with authority. "We'll know right away if the Captain is on to them." Rose smiled to herself. "Once he finds out, James will be done. Over. Finished." She probably would have continued providing synonyms about ending someone for at least another ten minutes if Sloane hadn't jumped in.

"Do you ever wonder what really happened that night?" It was a dangerous question, but Sloane knew there was no one else she could ask.

The smile on Rose's face faded. "Every day." Her dark eyes burned into Sloane's.

"He doesn't remember." Sloane's voice was barely above a whisper. "He wanted me to tell you that he doesn't remember."

Rose's face went white, her eyes wide. Sloane found herself standing. Her knees wobbled. She wanted to bolt from this bedroom before she broke apart into pieces. Nothing made sense anymore. Not James or Rose or the watches or the Gregorys. And this time there was no one to help her cheat, no geek she could pay to tell her the truth and make her look smart. This time Sloane was on her own. The fresh tears in Rose's eyes confirmed it.

"I should go," Sloane said.

"Yes," Rose choked out. "You should."

Chapter 23

First the repair. Then the packaging. Sloane had sent the watches as promised to the highest bidder, omitting a return address. An anonymous account had been created, the money transferred and withdrawn, only to be tucked back into the safety deposit box where it belonged. The score had been evened; what was lost to Mari was returned by the Captain. Over the past five days, Sloane had followed all the rules. Yet she felt emptier and more confused than ever. Maybe that's because the only thing left for the girls to do was watch the boys and wait for the other shoe to fall.

Rose offered a hand to Sloane as they climbed the jagged rocks lining the beach. "How do you even know he'll be here?" she whispered, swiping her hand across her forehead. "Doesn't he usually hang around the Club during the day?"

Sloane knew because ever since her collision with James at the driving range, she'd felt a pull she couldn't explain and kept ending up on the beach. And without fail she'd spot him there, punishing himself. Sometimes he sat for hours, staring at the great expanse of blue. Other days he'd run the rocky shoreline only to return an hour later, his face dripping with sweat or tears; Sloane could never be sure which. She suspected both. It looked an awful lot like penance. The silence. The running. The drinking. On repeat. She promised herself that she'd report to Madge, explain her findings, and inquire if Trip's behavior mirrored James's. If they were both self-destructing maybe the girls should just sit back and enjoy the show. Maybe it would be safer that way.

Today James was stripped bare. Literally.

Sloane and Rose crouched low, peering from behind the rocks. He lay face up on the sand, no blanket beneath him, completely naked. The sun beat down on his body, sweat beaded on his chest. He was still.

"Should we . . ." Rose's light brown skin had turned pink. "I mean, do you think he's okay?"

Sloane knew she should hate Rose for whatever history she had with James. After all, Willa was in love with him, too. It was her one big flaw, her one true weakness. Willa Ames-Rowan wasn't perfect, either. She'd always had a crush on him, and this year it had seemed more heightened, more acute somehow. But Sloane had to admit they made sense together. She couldn't say the same for Rose and James. They came from completely different worlds. Not exactly a solid foundation on which to build a relationship. Sloane knew a thing or two about faking and passing. In the end, it destroyed you from the inside.

"He's always out here. Ever since . . ." Sloane let her words trail away.

James struggled to push up on his elbows, sand clinging to his back. He unearthed his cell phone from the pile of clothes strewn next to him, dropping it into the sand once and retrieving it. After rubbing his eyes, he stumbled to his feet to dress in his shorts and T-shirt.

Cautiously, the girls followed. In his state, they didn't even have to keep that much of a distance. James was completely wasted as he lurched back toward the Club. Sloane couldn't help but wonder if there was someone who cared enough to escort him home, to put water by the side of his bed and wait until he sobered up to work through the entire, tangled mess. But no one seemed to notice. No one waved or smiled or stopped to chat, not even when James struggled at the gate, his body leaning into the iron. No one questioned him when he laughed hysterically after pushing into the French doors when he should have been pulling.

But Sloane knew there were whispers. They followed him everywhere he went. Hushed words about his sobriety, his grandfather, and his guilt. Sloane would self-destruct, too, if whispers followed her like a shadow. That's why she guarded her secrets so closely. Theoretically she'd actually have to say something out loud in order for people to start whispering about her. Being quiet was safer. Smarter.

James stumbled by Rory O'Neil on the back terrace. Rory smirked as he passed. Sloane's eyes narrowed. He was sitting with a girl wearing large, black sunglasses, her thick hair arranged into an oversized bun on top of her head. God only knew what he was up to. She slowed.

Rose pulled Sloane's arm toward a different entrance. Apparently she was avoiding the table as well.

"Liu!" Too late. Sloane pretended not to hear. She gulped when Rose scrunched her forehead in confusion. She had no pills for Rory's sister and hoped he'd get the hint and leave her alone.

"What does he want with *you*?" Rose whispered. "Stay

away from him. You saw him in those pictures Lina took. He's a drug dealer."

Sloane just shook her head, hanging close to Rose. But as she gripped the ornate handle of Hawthorne Lake's French doors, Rose's words echoed in her brain. The picture Lina took. James paying Rory on the basketball courts. "*Drug dealer. Drug dealer. Drug dealer.*"

"I'm going after James," Rose hissed. "Ditch Rory."

Sloane raced down the hall alone, fleeing Rory's insistent "Liu. Liu!" At least Rose wouldn't have a hard time trailing James. He dropped breadcrumbs in the form of a tipped vase, some bills and change—even his cell phone—which Sloane watched Rose bend to retrieve before she rounded a corner out of sight.

"*What do you have for me? This is good shit, Liu. Nice work.*"

The words played on repeat. Sloane had to steady herself against the wall, the knots in her stomach twisting when she visualized the picture Lina had snapped. James handing money to Rory. He couldn't be . . . They couldn't have been . . . They weren't hers . . .

"*What do you have for me? This is good shit, Liu. Nice work.*"

Rory's voice added even more knots, sharp pain shooting within her gut. Coupled with James's words, she doubled over.

"*I don't remember anything. I don't remember anything. I don't remember.*"

The walls shifted and began to close in on her. She slid to the floor and fumbled for her phone, hands shaking. Slowly she typed the word "narcolepsy" into her search bar, unable to remember the name of the little white pills she'd given to Rory. In her mind, the medicine would be abused by nerds who wanted to stay up all night to study for some big exam. She reminded herself of this as her phone pulled up results, reminded herself that those little white pills would never make James forget, would never make Willa . . . she couldn't even finish her thought.

"What are you waiting for?" Rose peered around the corner, waving Sloane over. "This is it!"

Sloane shoved the phone back in her pocket and got to her feet. Her mind was in a fog. Rose wasn't alone. Lina and Madge stood near one of the windows. Nadia dusted baseboards and Kira washed walls around the corner. Every soldier in the War was here—right outside the Captain's office. It could only mean one thing. The Gregory clan had converged.

The Captain's office was obscene, more like a library really, with rows of rare books lining the mahogany shelves. The door was closed, but if they stood close enough, they could catch the gist of the conversation inside. Lina grinned wickedly. Sloane felt sick. But she smiled back, because it was easier. Because she had to.

"It's working, you guys!" Madge whispered. Her smile was too big. Sloane had never really understood what people meant by the term crazy eyes, but looking at Madge, she totally got it. Harsh words floated through the cracks as the Captain screamed about watches, family history, and pride. He yelled at the boys for getting into trouble and selling the watches. He yelled at them for having to buy them back. Trip's muffled voice was hard to understand, but Sloane could hear that he was confused, mumbling about theft and trying to convince his Grandpa that they hadn't done anything wrong. James, of course, was silent.

And then they heard a crack. And a whimper. And a crash. And James, slurring something.

It played like a movie in Sloane's head. She couldn't see it, but the violent noise told the story. First the Captain hit Trip, then Trip fell to his knees and James stepped forward to protect him. Although maybe the last part didn't happen, considering James's condition. Madge pushed her fingers to her lips to stifle laughter, and Lina's eyes grew round.

"It was stupid," James barked loudly. The girls pushed their ears closer to the door, to be sure they heard correctly. "We shouldn't have sold them. It was dumb and it won't happen again."

The Captain had some choice words to say in response, but even from behind the heavy wood, they all knew the worst was over. The boys were off the hook, yet again.

Sloane couldn't work out how she felt. She knew she should be furious, but she was kind of relieved that James hadn't been disinherited because of their stupid prank. Part of her felt like this whole situation was spiraling out of control. What were they doing? Who were they punishing? Sloane forced herself to look into the eyes of her friends. They all looked tired. They were losing the War.

"Maybe this is a sign," she whispered.

Madge didn't hear her, or maybe just pretended not to hear. She merely took a deep breath and said in a strong, clear voice, "We're going to need a new plan."

Nobody said a word. They all backed away from the door.

"But how do we even know for sure that James did it?" Rose whispered.

As soon as the words were out of her mouth, Sloane was scared for her.

Madge moved in for the kill. "We know because I saw him on a boat with my sister. And for the record, his asshole brother was the one who helped them both get into the life-boat. So, yeah. I'm pretty damn sure."

Rose just stood there. She looked Madge in the eye. Shockingly enough her cold silence seemed to work. When Madge spoke again, almost all of the frustration was gone.

"He did it, okay? And I need the people who killed my sister to pay. I just . . ." She grabbed Lina's hand and then Sloane's, begging Rose to understand. Rose placed her fingers on top. "I just need to make sure nothing like this ever happens again."

And in that moment, Sloane didn't need to read the Google search results on her phone or talk to Rory or research the drugs she'd given him. Because in that moment, the pieces clicked together with sickening finality. The reason James didn't remember anything about that night wasn't because he was drunk like everyone thought. It was because of Sloane and her inability to be honest with herself or her parents. It was because she gave pills to a messed-up busboy in an effort to make some stupid statement about who was in charge of her life.

Her arm involuntarily went to her stomach like she might be able to prevent her breakfast from forcing its way up her esophagus and out of her mouth. Luckily she made it to the nearest exit before losing everything in the bushes beside the door.

I killed Willa. I killed Willa. I killed Willa.

July 4th, 10:43 P.M.

"*Come on, Sloane! What are you so afraid of?*" *Willa stood on top of a table, dancing wildly to the band that was now covering the Beastie Boys.*

Classic Willa. Two beers and she channeled a scantily clad pop star. Sloane wondered what it must be like to be fearless, to dance on tables and not worry about falling off or singing the wrong lyrics to the song at the top of her lungs. Sloane would never forget the slumber party last summer where she'd sang, "Hold me closer, Tony Danza. Count the head lice on the highway . . ." *to an old Elton John song. Lina still wouldn't let her live it down. The most fearless thing she'd done all night was hit* IGNORE *on the phone that vibrated in her pocket.*

The boat rocked dangerously, and Sloane skidded into something, or as it turned out, someone, dancing right behind her. His body was sweaty, and he grinded his lower half against hers in rhythm to the music.

Sloane's cheeks were already on fire when she looked back to see Trip Gregory's lopsided grin.

"What up, Liu? I have a thing for Asians, you know."

Sloane pried his hands off her waist and jerked away from him. As far as she knew, as far as everyone knew, Trip Gregory had a thing for just about every girl. Sloane glanced back up at Willa, swaying to the music, her eyes trained on the doorway across the room. She'd be no help. Willa was on a mission; it was almost as if she'd made James the leading man in one of her romance novels, and she was willing to do just about anything to make sure they got their happy ending. So far James seemed immune to Willa's charms, but no one could resist her for long. Besides, landing James would make her friend happy, and that was enough to make Sloane happy, too. But that didn't mean she wanted anything to do with Trip. Sloane jerked away.

"Hey, hey, not so fast." She felt his sweaty hands circle her waist again.

Before she could protest, he'd lifted her onto the table next to Willa.

"Woohoo! It's about time you got her up here. Nice work, Gregory!" Willa shrieked and giggled while Sloane stood next to her, unable to shake the paralyzing feeling of hundreds of eyes on her. In reality, no one had stopped dancing or had even noticed her standing next to Willa.

"Here, this will help you relax." Trip slipped a tiny white pill into her hand.

She glanced down at its round, white form. It looked almost exactly like the narcolepsy pills she'd given to Rory for his sister. If she remembered the definition, she might have thought it ironic. But she didn't, so she just pretended to swallow the pill but tossed it over her shoulder into the crowd of writhing bodies instead.

Trip hoisted himself onto the table and started moving against Willa with the music. Sloane watched as he jokingly told her to "open wide." She watched as he placed the pill on her tongue. Watched as Willa swallowed it with a bright smile.

Sloane slid down from the table, resigning herself to baby-sitting duty again. Not that she really minded. Babysitting her friend was easier than pretending to be cool and smart and whatever else she was supposed to be.

She felt an arm pulling on her elbow.

"Hey, have you seen my . . ." Madge noticed Willa dancing on the table, took in her bloodshot eyes and watched her sway dangerously with Trip. She sighed heavily and again turned to Sloane. "Great. That's just great. How long has she been like that?"

"On the table? Or wasted?" Sloane asked the first two questions that popped into her head and regretted them as soon as she saw Madge roll her eyes. She was in one of her moods.

"Willa! WILLA!" Madge shrieked over the pounding beat.

No response. Then again, if Willa were ignoring her step-sister completely, it wouldn't have come as a huge surprise to Sloane. The two had been arguing lately. She wasn't sure what was going on, but something had shifted between them. They didn't laugh together the way they used to.

Madge reached up to grab her sister and drag her down from the table, but Willa shook her arm away. "Leave me alone, Madge. I'm actually having some fun for once."

"You think this is fun? You're making a fool of yourself." Madge shouted over the music, and again, Willa pretended not to hear.

"*James!*" *Willa squealed.*

She hopped off the table and leaned dangerously toward Sloane who placed her hands on her shoulders, stabilizing her. "*He's going to kiss me,*" *Willa slurred.* "*I can feel it.*" *She squeezed Sloane's hand.* "*This is it, Sloaney. This is my night.*"

Sloane patted her shoulder awkwardly. She needed some air. Now that Madge had taken over as babysitter, Sloane did her best Houdini and headed out the nearest exit. She was good at disappearing when she needed to. She'd duck out of dances at school and linger in the bathroom, wander upstairs at parties only to sit on the edge of a bed in a quiet room. She'd even leave movies early, walk the dark sidewalks surrounding the theater and slip back in before the credits rolled.

Tonight, she managed to find a spot on the lower deck that was relatively quiet and settled into one of the cushy lounge chairs. The stars were bright in the summer sky. In that moment she felt small, tiny. It was comforting in a way. If the universe was infinite, that meant she really could be unnoticeable. After years of obsessive parents hovering over her, Sloane relished the thought of fading away into nothingness.

And as if someone was trying to prove her point or maybe test her theory, Willa and James ran out onto the deck in front of her. They didn't even glance at Sloane's chair in the shadows. When Willa reached up onto her tippy toes to kiss James in the moonlight, she didn't feel Sloane's eyes on her. And when Trip helped them into a small motorboat together, neither of them turned. Not even when Sloane stood up and began yelling at them to wait. They were drunk; it was late. They'd get themselves killed. No . . . Willa and James took off into the night oblivious to the girl in the shadows begging them to stay.

Sloane got up to go find Madge or Lina or someone who could help her figure out what to do next. She heard the fireworks exploding in the distance as she scoured the faces in the crowd for her friends. But it wasn't until long after the last burst—when she found a soaking wet James Gregory and pale-looking Lina cowering in the exact same chair where she'd hidden an hour earlier—that she knew something had gone very, very wrong.

PART 4

F.U.B.A.R.
(F***ed Up Beyond All Recognition)

Chapter 24

It was exactly 5.34 miles from the Ames-Rowan house to Hawthorne Lake.

Madge knew this because she and Willa made their dad drive it once when they were in seventh grade so they'd know the exact mileage of their daily bike rides. Madge remembered sitting in the Jag, watching the odometer creep upward, Willa's twelve-year-old voice cheering the needle on. Willa had burrowed her head into the seat of the car, as if she still couldn't get used to the smell of expensive leather. She'd grin from ear to ear when Madge's father would ruffle her blonde hair—as if to remind her that he was real, solid, and that he wasn't going to disappear like her biological dad.

At first Madge had been jealous of the way her father doted on her stepsister. But in the third grade, Willa had dedicated her first novel, *My Only Home,* (illustrated with Crayolas and handwritten in careful cursive) to her new stepsister, Madge. It was basically a love letter to Madge and her dad, with the names changed. That day, a tiny piece of Madge's heart that had frozen after her mother died, began to thaw. Willa had this way of making people melt. Now that she was gone, Madge wondered who would soften the grief that crystallized there now.

So instead of waiting around for someone else to save her, Madge was doing her best to save herself. Her body screamed at her to stop running. Her pounding, frozen heart begged her to slow down, but Madge kept on, the key on the chain around her neck pinging against her chest. One foot in front of the other. Her legs cut through the thick July air, so humid it felt like she was running through the middle of the lake.

So close.

Madge had almost tasted their blood. Maybe Sloane was right. Maybe she should give up. She knew they were never going to win, but she'd never lost before Willa died. Not really. She was captain of the debate team, student council president, and an all-state tennis champion. Failure was not on option. Not for Madge. And definitely not when it came to making things right for Willa.

Her lungs burned, and her tank top clung to her stomach, drenched with sweat. She jogged past Magnolia Park and saw the water fountain wavy in the heat near the playground. She imagined how good the cool water would feel on her lips, trickling down her throat, but she was almost home. She'd left the Club determined not to stop. And just as determined, Madge jogged right past it.

People make a lot of assumptions when your sister dies. They assume your life is a mess. They assume your parents' lives are falling apart. They can almost smell the quiet on you. They hear it in the rasp of your voice; they feel it in your desperation for human contact. They observe your borderline compulsive need to surround yourself with people who help you learn to forget instead of ones who force you to remember. When your sister dies, people look at you like you died, too. In a lot of ways they're right, Madge realized. She was dead. All the important parts of her, anyway.

A grim smile twisted Madge's lips when she turned onto her street and saw her stepmother's Porsche parked in the driveway. It was one of the many things Carol Ames-Rowan not-so-subtly hinted that she wanted or needed or had to have. Madge's father wasn't in the business of saying no. And his yeses were over-the-top, like some cheesy commercial for doting husbandry. There'd be a new car in the driveway with a red bow around it or a scavenger hunt to find the bracelet Willa's mother had been drooling over that month. In the year before Willa died, Madge's credit card had been declined, and the money from her bank account drained. It wasn't difficult to identify the blue-eyed, blonde-haired root of the problem. But miraculously the Ames-Rowan's financial crisis disappeared right along with Willa. Or maybe her father had just figured out how to hide his problems better.

Carol and Willa had been a package deal, so Madge had always managed to hide just how much she loathed Carol. Well, most of the time. But now that Willa was gone, there was a new friction between the two. Madge realized that most days she felt like some kind of hate-seeking missile, just looking for the right person to target and destroy. Still, she couldn't help herself. So when she tore into the kitchen after running the 5.34 miles home from the Club, the perfect target sat right in her line of fire.

"Honey! What's happened?" Carol dropped the magazine she was reading and stood. "I've tried calling."

Madge rolled her eyes and turned toward the laundry

room for a towel. "I just went for a run. Call off the search party, Carol."

"It's almost a hundred degrees outside. Are you crazy?" Her stepmother grabbed a bottled water from the fridge and held it out to Madge.

"I was at the Club. No one could drive me home," she lied. Her friends had insisted on giving her a lift, but she'd remained steadfast as she pulled the sports bra over her head and laced up her running shoes in the locker room. She needed to clear her head. She wouldn't have cared if it were a thousand degrees.

Madge twisted the cap off the water but only allowed herself a tiny sip. It was a game she played, even when Willa was still alive. Minimal gratification. She'd download a new favorite song, but wouldn't allow herself to listen to it. Or she'd bake a batch of chocolate chip cookies and ration a tiny corner of a warm cookie as a reward. Watching her friends devour the rest took willpower. Playing with deprivation made her stronger. The wanting. And not having.

Carol eyed her with worry or anger or both, and Madge felt a fresh rush of satisfaction. That clinched it. She wouldn't drink the rest of that water. In fact, she wished she had the energy to run another lap around her neighborhood. That would really piss Carol off.

"How are the girls doing?" her stepmother finally asked, retreating back to her magazine at the table with dead eyes.

Several weeks ago, Madge had overheard Carol whispering with her father that if she could just get Madge to open up to her that maybe she'd stop being so angry all the time. Classic Carol: she believed *she* could solve anything. What her stepmother didn't understand—would never understand—was that Madge wanted to be angry. She needed the anger.

As long as she was angry, she didn't have time to wallow in grief. She didn't have time to think about the empty room next to hers or the way her sister's flip-flops were still tucked under Madge's bed in exactly the same position she'd left them more than four weeks ago.

Only now, she couldn't help but think about Willa, because Carol was sitting in her chair. She'd claimed it without explanation since Willa's death, like it had never been anyone else's. Something about the sight of her stepmother's bony ass in that chair set Madge's blood on fire. Carol usually had a magazine or a book, but Madge knew she wasn't reading the pages. She'd watch as the shell of a woman stared into space, the same page displayed in front of her day after day after day. In her dead daughter's spot at the table.

"Madge? I asked you a question." Carol didn't look up from the unread page. She sounded more like an annoyed babysitter than a stepmother, which pretty much summed up their entire relationship.

Instead of responding, Madge took a tin from the counter drawer and placed a mint delicately in her mouth. First she flattened the mint on her tongue. Then she twirled it once to the left, twice to the right, and flattened once again. She continued this rhythm as she shut the lid with a satisfying click. It was her post-Willa routine. Anytime she started to feel like she might lose it, she put a mint in her mouth. The reason was simple: they reminded her of Willa's funeral. Carol and her father had practically force-fed them to her the entire time she stood in the ridiculous receiving line at her sister's wake. To Madge, the round little peppermints tasted of tears and strangers' hugs and her sister's ashes all rolled into one. Whenever she needed a reminder of what she was doing or why she had to keep going, she'd pop one in her mouth. Nothing like the taste of death to light a fire under your ass.

"Madge, how are the girls?" Carol repeated, her voice sharpening. "I miss seeing them now that . . ." Her stepmother trailed off. They did that a lot now. Let their voices fade to nothing.

"They're dealing." It was a lie. They both knew it. Besides, Madge wasn't even sure what the truth really was, only that Lina and Sloane were operating with a broken compass. Willa had been their true North, and now that she was gone, neither had known where to go or whom to follow. Madge had no choice but to take action. She'd begun the War with the sole purpose of ruining the Gregorys' lives the same way that they'd ruined hers, but the reality was that it gave the girls a purpose, a sense of direction. It also brought out their worst, which Willa had never done. Lina was even more prone to cruelty and Sloane had retreated even further into herself. Every once in a while, Madge still caught flashes of her old friends. The spark of pleasure in Lina's eyes after they had orchestrated the hand off of the Gregorys' watches. The quiet pride in Sloane's voice when she'd come up with the watch idea in the first place. Brief moments that reminded Madge that though her best friends now seemed like strangers, the girls she remembered were in there somewhere.

And then, of course, there was Rose.

Madge didn't know her at all before she'd barged into the attic on that first day. She'd seen her around with Willa, of course, but that never meant much to Madge. Willa was nice to everyone, plucked rejects like some girls gathered shoes off the sales rack at Nordstrom. All of them were eligible, even the ones that had spent far too long on the shelf. Madge always thought it was dangerous letting people in, particularly Rose with her sneaky mother who was always pushing her daughter in front of the members at Club events. The social climber never fell far from the ladder.

But Rose wasn't like that. She turned out to be a living, breathing reminder of why Willa's philosophy sometimes paid off. To Rose, Willa's friendship was nothing more than friendship, and the War was an opportunity to seek justice. Besides, in a way, Madge's response to Carol was actually the truth depending on how you looked at it. Like so many other things in life, "dealing" existed on a spectrum. Her remaining friends were all still speaking to one another. And they'd live to fight another day. If that wasn't dealing, she wasn't sure what was.

"I'm going to take a shower." Madge marched up to her room. After flinging her sweaty clothes across the floor, she turned the water on so cold that the spray felt like tiny needles across her bare skin. She refused to arch her back away from the stream or even let herself gasp beneath the freezing water. Each icy drop made her a little stronger, adding a little numbness to the sadness that always lingered around the edges. The pain cleared Madge's head of the uncertainty that had crept in since the girls' most recent failure.

A new plan formed. And with it, steely resolve.

She quickly dried herself off, dressed, and sent a text.

War meeting tonight at 9 P.M. Same place.

She included their newest recruits, even though Kira and Nadia still made Madge uncomfortable. If she was being honest with herself, she'd ignored the staff the same way the Gregorys ignored them. She never knew their names or bothered to say "please" or "thank you." She left that up to Willa.

But when Kira and Nadia had appeared, devastated with the story of their own sister, her whole world shifted a little on its axis. And now when she saw the girl behind the bar with her cheap vanilla lotion, she wondered what her parents were like. If she had dreams. A scholarship. A sister. But the discomfort of being around Kira and Nadia also sparked ideas of something bigger than what she'd begun plotting the moment her sister was pulled from the lake. Kira and Nadia represented what could be a revolution, something that could change Hawthorne Lake forever, long after the Gregorys were gone.

The first reply didn't come until 7:12 P.M. Fewer than two hours before they were supposed to meet. Madge was in bed, staring at the ceiling.

Sorry, fam dinner before parents leave.

Lina.

Madge drew air into her lungs, holding it long enough to feel it burn. Her dad liked to remind her how she used to throw epic tantrums as a toddler, holding her breath until she turned blue. So much for evolution.

Sloane's response came ten minutes later.

Mandatory hospital hang out. Rain check.

Madge ground her teeth and ran her finger over Willa's initials engraved in her key.

And finally Rose's.

Let's do breakfast instead. Ivy room at the Club. Kira, Nadia wrking. Will catch up ltr.

No meeting. No attic. No maids. No War. Rose's text smelled an awful lot like an intervention. Madge's pulse quickened. She jumped up and shut the blackout blinds on her windows, bathing her room in blackness. Only in the dark would she call a truce; only when she could barely see her hand in front of her face would she quit the game. Instead of biting back tears, she'd finally let them slip down her cheeks.

Chapter 25

Madge must have fallen asleep because the next time she opened her eyes, the clock read 8:42 P.M. Night leaked beneath the edges of her blinds. Her head felt achy, her room hot and cramped. She needed fresh air and a sip of water. But when she crept downstairs, she found the lights blazing in her father's office.

"So everything is in order? The first installment processed?" He was whispering, hunched over his desk. She didn't need to see her father's face to know that his forehead was crinkled with worry. She could tell by the slump in his shoulders that he wasn't as optimistic as he was trying to sound. "Well, great. That's good news." He raked a hand through his wiry grey hair. He was lying.

Money had never been an issue for the Ames-Rowan family. Private school, country clubs, exotic vacations, and cars that cost more than houses: that was pretty much the norm in their household. At least it had been until her father invested his entire inheritance in some doomed hedge fund.

"Yes, I believe the payments will be arriving on a semi-annual basis in accordance with our agreement." Her father swiveled around in his desk chair and saw Madge standing there hanging on his every word. His face went pale beneath his perma golf tan. He seemed to instantly age another ten years. "I'm sorry; I'll have to call you back." He placed the phone in the cradle.

Neither spoke.

"Just working out the details of a new deal." He tried to smile, but the corners of his mouth stretched into a grimace instead. "I only wish . . . the timing." His voice broke on the last word.

Madge just stared back at him. What could he possibly want her to say? That if he hadn't lost all of their money then maybe his batshit crazy wife wouldn't have tried to marry off his stepdaughter to a Gregory? Madge often wondered if her father was able to see the connection between their money problems, his wife, and the changes in Willa. But the new lines on his face told her everything she needed to know. Her father knew he had Willa's blood on his hands.

He stood and stepped to her, placing his hands on her shoulders.

"Everything is better now. I promise." His dry lips grazed her forehead. She wanted to scream and yell that nothing was ever going to be better. She wanted to tell her father that he'd ruined everything. But there was a tiny hole in the arm of his golf shirt and less hair on his head. There was no way that Madge could tell this stooped, broken man what he already knew.

"I'm gonna meet the girls at the Club." It was another lie between them, but she had to get out of the house. She backed out of the office and made her way toward the garage.

"I can give you a ride. Just give me a minute," her father called after her.

But Madge ignored him and jumped onto her bike, pedaling out the open garage door as fast as she could. Stars hung above her in the night sky, and she made up a wish for Willa. When the girls were little, Willa would squeeze her eyes shut, her lips moving, the sound trapped inside. Madge had a knack for guessing each of her sister's wishes—a bright pink bike, a trampoline, horseback riding lessons. She'd taunt Willa with their closeness, Madge knew her like no one else, and Willa would pretend to get mad. In the end, though, they'd laugh until they cried. Tonight, Madge decided, Willa would wish for justice.

Droplets of water glittered on sprawling lawns beneath the moonlight giving the properties a sort of sparkle. Each of the houses looked so perfect from the sidewalk, amber light spilling from walls of windows. They looked like the kind of places where nothing bad could ever happen. But Madge had learned that houses, like people, did fine jobs of concealing the lies within them.

There would be no War meeting tonight, but still Madge found herself pedaling to Hawthorne Lake. She needed the comfort and privacy of the attic. It was the only place where she could think these days.

When she turned into the Club's long and winding drive she thought again about when she and Willa had decided to ride their bikes to the Club for the first time. They had spent almost the entire summer trying to talk her dad and Carol into letting them go. Their parents were full of excuses. *"It's too long. There aren't streetlights. You'll get tired and end up in a ditch on the side of the road."* Until finally, on Labor Day weekend, Madge made the executive decision that they should just do it. The girls waited until Carol was in the shower and Madge's dad was dozing in front of some golf tournament on TV. They snuck into the garage and strapped on their pink bike helmets.

"Are you sure we should . . ." Madge saw fear in Willa's blue eyes but she refused to let her finish. The less time they spent thinking about this the better.

"Race ya." Madge stepped on the pedals of her baby blue Huffy and took off down the driveway.

She felt like she was flying.

Willa was in her shadow the whole way to the Club, and Madge spent most of her ride looking over her shoulder for her dad's silver car. They were almost there. Home free. But just as they pulled their bikes onto the winding drive that led to the Club, Willa took the corner wrong and ended up sprawled across the concrete. Madge was off her bike and at her sister's side in seconds. Willa sobbed. Her knees and elbows bled. Madge tried to help Willa to her feet, but she refused to budge.

"I'm not going anywhere. This was a terrible idea. Call your dad and have him pick me up."

"But if we call, they'll never let us ride together again. We have to do this. If we can ride to the Club we can go swimming whenever we want and play tennis and . . ."

But Willa already had her phone out, fat tears sliding down her cheeks. "I fell. Madge thought we should ride to the Club. I need you to come get me."

Madge didn't speak to her for days.

It was ridiculous in retrospect. A waste of valuable time with Willa. But seeing the Club sign and riding up the brick paved drive never failed to remind Madge of Willa lying on the ground. Crying. Weak. Unable to pick herself up. Madge always looked at the spot where Willa fell when she rode by, even when Willa was alive. Until it rained, the bloodstains remained on the concrete, but they'd washed away long ago, and even if they hadn't, it would be too dark to see them tonight. But as she came up on the turn, she caught movement out of the corner of her eye.

There in the bushes right next to the Club's sign was Trip Gregory on top of some nondescript blonde.

Madge felt a fresh wave of rage roll through her body. Now she'd never be able to ride past the Club's entrance and remember Willa and her stupid injury. Yet another memory of her sister stolen by a Gregory. She was barely conscious of tossing her bike aside and sneaking past the after-dinner guests, storming up the narrow stairwell to the attic. But she stopped short of the top step.

"I'm worried about her." The high-pitched, soft-spoken voice belonged to Sloane.

Madge's hand flew to the doorknob. What the hell did they think they were doing meeting without her?

"It almost seems like she's in some kind of denial."

Lina. Madge's hand dropped. Who was Lina to psychoanalyze her? Unfreakingbelievable. If anyone was in denial it was Lina, and it had absolutely nothing to do with what happened to Willa.

"Well, I'm just not sure we're fighting the right people anymore." Rose's voice was louder and rang with a new authority. "I spoke to James and it turns out he doesn't even remember what happened that night. I'm not sure he was even . . ."

Madge threw open the door before Rose could finish.

"Sorry, I'm late."

The girls gaped at her, their faces stunned. She flashed an icy smile and closed the door calmly, as if she'd called the meeting herself. Which, for the record, she had.

"I'm so glad you guys were able to figure out a way to get here. I didn't think you were going to make it." Madge made a point of looking directly into each of their faces. None of them met her eyes. Not even Lina.

Rose shook her head, wringing her fingers together in knots. "It's over," she blurted.

Lina nodded approvingly. Sloane looked like she might cry.

Madge felt nothing but quivering rage. These were her friends and this was her club; no one was going to shut it down before *she* was ready. "No." She didn't need a mint this time, didn't need to imagine Willa's funeral or think of her broken family pretending to be normal. "I have a new idea: their cars. I can't believe I hadn't thought of it before. It's perfect."

The girls remained still, as if they'd just realized they were on the wrong end of the firing squad. A feeling of déjà vu crept up Madge's spine like clammy fingers. She had seen this look before. She remembered it vividly on Willa's face after Madge had told Carol she wasn't going to be a bridesmaid in her ridiculous vow renewal ceremony. More recently she'd seen it on her father's face when he caught her sleeping in Willa's bed again; on the same day she'd demanded to know why he let Carol sit in Willa's chair at the kitchen table. It was a look that said she had problems that were too big for anyone to fix.

But Madge ignored them and barreled onward, fueled by a renewed sense of purpose. "I mean it's such an obvious solution. They love their stupid cars. There are so many options!" She continued rambling about scratches, dents, slashing tires, and messing with the brothers' famous drag races, staging a hit-and-run, pulling stop signs. She couldn't stop. The words tumbled from her mouth, the ideas spewing like the lake

water from around her sister's blue lips as the EMT pumped
her chest.

"Madge!" Lina rasped.

She jumped up and grabbed Madge's hand, squeezing it in
her own. Amazing that Lina's fingers could be so soft when
the rest of her was so hard. Sloane sniffled and stood as well,
taking Madge's other hand. Rose lowered her head. It was as
though they were performing a vigil. It made Madge want to
kill someone.

"It's time to go, Madge." Lina opened the door.

"I'm not leaving." The truth was Madge had nowhere to
go. She wasn't about to return home. And she had no desire
to hang out by the pool, watching people couple off in dark
corners. Outside of this attic, Madge had nothing.

Sloane choked back another sob. Clearly Madge was
freaking her out. Lina threw a protective arm around Sloane's
shoulder and exchanged a look with Rose. Rose nodded and
stood as the other two girls made their way down the stairs.

"So . . . maybe we could talk? They're worried about you,
you know." Rose started blowing out the candles one by one.

But Madge ignored her, ignored the concern in her voice,
and focused on the search results on her phone. This new
plan was real and possible. She had to prove it to them. She
had to make it happen tonight before she lost her nerve. "I
need you to take me somewhere. It's important."

Rose paused for a second, considering her options. "Fine.
But only if you promise me you'll talk to someone about all
of this. Deal?"

"Deal."

Chapter 26

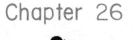

In silence, the two made their way back to the employee lot, far from the shiny Jags and Porsches, where Rose had parked her Dad's old Ford.

"Where to?"

"The Gregorys' house." Madge fastened her seatbelt and stared straight ahead.

Rose's knuckles went white on the steering wheel. "Madge, it's late. My parents will freak."

"I get it," Madge lied. "I know this has to stop. But they killed my sister, Rose. Either you take me to their house or I'll find another way. I could really use a friend right now."

It felt strange to plead with someone like Rose. She had to tread carefully.

Finally Rose sighed and started the car. She hesitated at the entrance to Hawthorne Lake, and Madge could almost hear her negotiating with her conscience. Rose just wanted to drive her home. But as the car idled, Madge knew Rose felt a pull in another direction that she couldn't ignore. It tugged at the possibility of a friendship, and Madge knew Rose didn't want to pass that up. Not when she'd finally found a place where she belonged. Her hand hovered over the blinker but finally fell away. Rose drove straight.

"I'm not getting out," she said. "Do what you have to do. This is it. You get one last chance to bury this, Madge." She turned down the private lane, ancient oak trees canopied above them creating a leafy green tunnel. Halfway down the road, she flicked her lights off and slowed in front of the Gregorys' sprawling estate. "I'll pull halfway up, but you have to walk the rest of the way. If you're not back in ten minutes, I'm leaving." Rose stared straight ahead. Madge wondered if she'd even have the nerve.

"I'll be back in five."

She gently opened the door of the car and left it open an inch to avoid a slam, then jogged up the driveway to Trip's car. Pulling her phone from her pocket, she clicked to review the photo again: BMW brake systems. Her plan was barely thought-through, but sometimes those were the best kind. She'd had all of five minutes in the car to prepare, but as she knelt beside Trip's shiny car and used her phone to illuminate the underside, she felt confident that she'd complete her mission. How hard could pulling a brake line be? She gripped the closest thing to a brake hose that she could find and pulled gently at first. Nothing happened. She pulled harder and finally had to grip the line with two hands, anchoring her feet to the cement in order to pull with all her strength.

"Madge!" Rose was out of her car and storming up the driveway. "What the hell are you doing?" Even in the darkness, Madge could see the horror and disgust in her eyes.

"I said I'd be back in five minutes. Just give me five

minutes!" Madge felt sweat bead along her forehead and yanked again on the line. Nothing.

And then the driveway was bathed in a light so white and bright and shocking, it might as well have been some tunnel to the afterlife. Madge would have almost welcomed death. Right now, it seemed like a better option than being caught by James Gregory. He cut the lights and the engine and stumbled out of his car. With a strange smile, he narrowed his eyes and cocked his head in front of the garage.

Madge jumped to her feet, wiping her black fingers down the length of her summer dress. His eyes landed first on the greasy streaks and then on her face as though he couldn't quite connect the two together. Then he turned to Rose. Madge swore she saw something inside him break. His lips quivered; he blinked rapidly. She catalogued the expression in her mind and focused on retaining every detail so she could call it up when she needed it the most.

"That's not even the right one," he said.

Rose and Madge exchanged a glance. She looked as sick and scared as Madge felt. James nodded to his brother's car. But something about the way he said the words made it clear he'd given up, surrendered. If Madge were being honest, she knew he hadn't even bothered fighting to begin with.

"If you want me dead so bad, you should at least do your research."

"James . . ." Rose whispered his name, but by the time it left her lips, he'd disappeared into the house.

Movement in one of the upstairs windows caught Madge's eye. The Captain? Trip? Did it even matter? She turned back to the expensive car, the brake line intact. It took all she had not to bend down and continue what she'd started. She knew it was Trip's car. He was the one she was really after. The one she really wanted to hurt. And as hard as she tried to tell herself it was truly over, she couldn't stop her brain from reeling, planning. She wasn't sure anything would ever be enough.

July 4th, 10:52 P.M.

"*Get off the damn table, Willa.*"

Madge yanked her sister's leg. At this point she didn't care if Willa bit it in front of their entire group of friends. Enough was enough.

Sloane shrugged. There was nothing she could do, either. Her soft voice could never be heard over the music.

"*Now!*" *Madge barked.*

"*Not until you come and get me!*" *Willa giggled and spun around next to Trip Gregory. She looked like a spoiled child, like an idiot. She was head over heels in love with her life. Madge swallowed back jealousy, wondering if she'd ever look that free or feel that happy. And then Willa stopped dancing. She might as well have had stars in her eyes.* "*James!*" *she cried.*

Willa jumped down from the table, stopping only to whisper to Sloane and then flew right out of their grasp like a hummingbird.

James kept a polite distance from Willa, the same way he did whenever any girl threw themselves at him. But she never grew discouraged. Madge knew why: Willa believed in that trashy crap she read. If James was a character in one of the romance novels she devoured on a daily basis, he'd come around. He'd stop drinking, breaking things, and otherwise behaving badly, and he'd fall in love with Willa. It wasn't a matter of if; it was a matter of when. Boys like James fell in love with girls like Willa. It was practically a law.

Madge watched her sister across the room, could see the sweet flush on her cheeks from where she stood. She watched as Willa lifted onto her tiptoes and slung her arms around James's strong shoulders. Willa appeared oblivious to his awkwardness, his resistance. Madge knew this would be one of those nights where Willa would sneak into her room and climb into her bed like she used to do all those years ago. Back when the two girls had first become a family.

Yes, tonight she'd be all nerves and excitement. Tonight she'd whisper into the dark about her dreams and ask her sister if she'd seen the look on James's face, if she'd felt it, too. Madge would roll her eyes, but at the same time relish every second. If that was what closeness with Willa meant these days, she'd take it. Like all the best things in life, it never lasted long enough.

Willa's laugh rose above the music. James barely even cracked a smile.

Madge saw through all of his bullshit. Why couldn't Willa? He was just another entitled brat living some kind of fantasy. But his fantasy was real life: he'd not only hit the genetic jackpot but was also filthy rich. Willa was too good for him. It was so easy to see what her future would look like with a boy like James. He'd never laugh at her goofy jokes; he'd probably force her to stop reading all of her trashy romance novels; there was no way he'd encourage her to follow her dream of writing a grown-up version of My Only Home *or doing celebrity interviews for* Teen Vogue. *No, if Willa fell in love with a guy like James she'd end up just like her mother. Bitter, sad, and destitute after her third husband gambled the family into a pit.*

No way would Madge let that happen to Willa. No way would Willa end up a forgotten trophy wife. So she marched over to her sister and decided to end this stupidity once and for all.

"Can I talk to you?" Madge stood with her back to James, refusing to even acknowledge his existence.

"'Course you can!" Willa chirped but didn't stop swaying to the beat.

"In private. I need to talk to you in private."

But Willa just kept dancing. Madge grabbed her arm and yanked her out onto the deck of the boat. Maybe some fresh air would do her good.

"You've had too much to drink. We should go."

"I'm not going anywhere. James and I are finally talking. I want to stay." She sang the words like a toddler, still swaying on her feet, even though there was no music. Her eyes were bleary and her words were slurred. This was worse than Madge thought.

"Come on, I've got to get you home."

"No way. You're not going to ruin this for me. Not tonight." Willa slithered out of Madge's grasp and started walking back toward the party. "You're just jealous. You hate seeing me happy. Well, sorry, Madge, I'm not going to spend the best years of my life moping around. I'd rather love and

lose or live and love." She paused and giggled. "Whatever. You know what I mean."

Madge knew exactly what she meant. She'd heard the same accusations out of Willa every time she tried to steer her away from James. And some of it was true. She was jealous. But she was also afraid of the way her stepmother encouraged Willa. She was afraid that on some twisted level, Carol was pulling the strings, coaxing her beautiful daughter to chase after the heir to the Hawthorne Lake empire.

"You are throwing yourself at some jackass," Madge spat. "Who isn't the least bit interested, for the record, all because you think it's what you're supposed to do." Her voice rose, but she couldn't stop the words from pouring out. "You're such a stereotype, Willa. Blonde, beautiful princess who thinks she's in love with a dark, handsome asshole, but really she's been manipulated and raised to think she should fall in love. Give it up. You reek of desperation. Or maybe it's eau de gold digger. Just like your mother."

Too far. She'd gone too far. Madge expected her sister to burst into tears. To slap her. To run away.

What she did not expect was for Willa to laugh in her face.

"You're so completely tragic, you know that?" The words came out jumbled-sounding. Willa was becoming more wasted by the minute despite the fact that Madge hadn't seen her take a sip. Willa spun on her heels and started back toward the party, but didn't make it more than four steps before falling in a puddle of drunk girl.

Trip appeared out of nowhere. "Whoa," he said, bending to Willa's side.

Shit. How long had he been there? What had he heard? Madge liked to think she didn't care about the Gregorys or *what they thought, but she did. It was impossible to be a member at the Club and not care about them.*

"Easy there, killer." Trip helped Willa back up into a standing position. "Hey, let's get you out of here . . ." He nodded at Madge.

She felt a slight sense of relief at having someone on her team. Maybe he'd step up and actually help get Willa home. Maybe he'd surprise her.

But then James stumbled onto the deck. Her face brightened as she slipped from beneath Trip's grasp, drawn to him like a magnet. Madge marveled at how much more drunk he appeared compared to a half hour ago. His light hair was mussed, his eyelids so heavy it was a wonder he could see. The transformation was dangerous. They laughed hysterically at each other as though Trip and Madge were invisible, which in a way they pretty much were. Eclipsed by their siblings.

"Keep an eye on her, Trip. I'm gonna grab my purse and get her home." Madge was ready to end the night. Trip wasn't the most responsible guy in the world, but surely he'd be able to keep an eye on Willa for five minutes while she grabbed her bag.

She should have known better.

As Madge ducked into a guest room to retrieve her purse, she heard the revving of a motorboat. She ran back out onto the deck just in time to see James driving the boat away.

Trip stood at the railing, screaming into the night. But his voice was nothing against the boat's motor.

"What the hell?" Madge shouted. "How could you have let them go?"

Trip was serious for once in his life, his normal grin replaced by confusion. "I tried to stop them, but you know

James. He's kind of impossible to stop when he decides he wants something." He grabbed Madge's arm and pulled her toward the stairs that led to the opposite end of the yacht. "Come on, there's another skiff over here. We'll get them back." Trip climbed in and started the engine, then lent a hand for Madge to follow. The narrow wood creaked and teetered under her heels. She quickly sat down before she fell over. "I know exactly where James takes girls. There's a sand-bar not too far from here. Guarantee they'll either be passed out or making out."

The boat bounced over the dark water. She felt queasy. The cool spray across her arms and legs did nothing to extinguish her anger. Willa was taking stupidity to a whole new level tonight, and Madge was sick of having to pick up the pieces. Without thinking, she snatched up her phone and texted: when i find u i'm gonna kill u. She almost hesitated—not because she regretted the words, but because she'd texted the exact same message dozens of time in the past and Willa always laughed it off. Madge could never sound serious enough. i mean it, she added, then pressed send.

"Sucks being the older sibling, right?" Trip laughed.

"Uh yeah, it does." She tucked her phone back in her bag. "But aren't you like five minutes younger than James or something?"

"Well, that depends on your source." Trip shook his head, his red hair catching in the moonlight. "According to my grandfather I'm younger, but my birth certificate says I was first."

"But why would they lie? I don't get it."

"Oh come on, you know how the story goes. He hates me. I'm the reason my parents are dead. In the old man's eyes I'm a killer." Trip's smile stopped at his eyes.

Madge wasn't sure how to respond to that. She twisted the chain of her key necklace around her finger. She'd heard the rumors about the head-on collision that killed his parents, but she'd never guessed they were actually true. Or maybe she'd found them too creepy to think about.

"And here are the little lovebirds now." Trip maneuvered over to where James's boat idled near a sand bar. From a distance it looked empty but as they pulled in closer, Madge could make out Willa and James lying in the bottom, not moving.

"Jesus, they passed out." Madge moved over to the edge and tried to get a better look. The boat rocked slightly beneath her weight, water lapping up around the side.

"Don't freak out. You know how to drive a boat, right?" Trip kicked off his shoes and climbed over the edge, the water rising to his knees as he waded to the other boat.

Madge nodded mutely.

"Great. I'll follow you back. Take it slow. It's dark."

"You sure?"

"I'm sure," Trip said. "Just get back to the yacht."

Madge swallowed. She nodded again and pushed the boat into gear. She was going to kill Willa for this. Literally strangle her. But maybe this was finally the wake-up call she needed. Maybe now she'd begin to see how stupid she was acting. Maybe she'd even realize that her mother was manipulating her.

Fireworks bloomed in the sky as Madge made her way back to the yacht. They were somehow even more beautiful from the quiet of the deep lake, the colors lingering in the dark sky long after another burst had taken its place. She felt a calmness wash over her, a bit of the anger finding its way out. She'd always loved fireworks. Ever since she was little. She and Willa would lay out on a blanket, bellies full of candy, glow-in-the-dark bracelets trailing up their arms. Willa would hold Madge's hand, scared of the loud noises. Madge's hand felt empty as she flew through the black water.

By the time she found her way back to the yacht, the show was over, but the party was still in full swing. She stood at the stern, watching for the little vessel that carried her sister. Her stomach twisted. What was taking them so long? A sick feeling of dread wormed its way into her throat.

After an eternity, she heard the engine.

She was down the stairs and next to the boat just in time to see Trip drag a semi-conscious James onto the yacht. She craned her neck. "Trip! Where's Willa?"

His eyes were wild when they met hers. He nearly dropped his brother. "She's not here? I was praying she was with you. She's not with you?" The words tumbled out of his mouth, each one bumping into the next. Madge had never heard him so scared, had never seen his face so warped.

"Trip? My sister? Where the hell is she?" She'd heard him wrong. This wasn't happening. She was face to face with him now. Or as close as she could get to his six-foot-four frame. He shook his head at her, his eyes flicking across the deck and behind her, forcing her to take a step back. "Willa." She whispered her name.

"My grandfather. We need to find my grandfather now!"

But instead of following Trip, Madge threw her bag aside, kicked off her shoes, and dove into the water. She swam back toward the sandbar in long practiced strokes. Willa was still there. She had to be. Her muscles burned and cried. It had taken five minutes by skiff. Maybe it took her five minutes swimming. Or an hour. She'd lost all sense of time. When Madge finally reached the sandbar, she waded onto the *shallow waters and sat down to wait for Willa to return. This was just one of the Gregorys' stupid practical jokes. Madge knew if she waited there long enough, Willa would show up giggling and make fun of her overly serious sister.*

So Madge waited. And waited.

The moon had practically set when the first of the search boats appeared. At first she struggled against the police who tried to pry her off her perch. She only stopped when she saw the men on one of the other boats fish her sister's body from the lake. She watched them try to revive her with chest pumps and mouth-to-mouth breathing. She watched them give up when Willa didn't respond.

Sometimes Madge still believed that if only they'd have left her alone out there a little longer, if only the Captain's search party had faced some sort of delay, Willa would have finally swum back to her. Just a few more minutes and she would have come back. Madge was sure of it.

PART 5

T.A.C.A.M.O.
Take Charge And Move Out

Chapter 27

Madge dreamt of a doorbell. It ripped through the thick silence on the beach. It clanged from Willa's blue lips. By the fourth ding, Madge shot up and found herself in bed, her heart slamming wildly in her chest. The previous night flooded over her, the look of disappointment etched across Rose's face. And as hard as Madge tried to dredge up a feeling of regret, as much as she tried to conjure up any type of guilt, she couldn't seem to muster either. Maybe she was just too tired.

The doorbell rang again.

Madge rubbed her eyes, trying to focus on the time on her phone and what the numbers meant. Her head finally cleared enough to comprehend that 7:26 A.M. meant it was too early for doorbells. She slipped on a bra under her T-shirt and poked her head out the door, gripping her phone like a weapon.

"Carol?" She waited a beat. "Dad?"

The doorbell sounded again. This time it sent a shudder

through her system. She knew she was alone—since Willa's funeral, she'd almost always found herself alone after 7 A.M.—and anyone could be standing behind that door. The house felt insubstantial, the walls too thin, a window easily broken, the alarm they never set, worthless. Madge ducked into Willa's room and pulled a tiny section of her curtain back to check the driveway. The window was cool on her cheek, the air conditioner on overdrive, and her breath fogged the glass. Lina's car was parked in front with Rose's close behind.

Her relief was short-lived. Sick regret began to consume her. She was awake now. She thought of the previous night, of the semi-out-of-body-experience she'd had when approaching the Gregorys' house—pulling on the brake line, the potential destruction it could have caused if everything had gone right. Or wrong, depending upon how you looked at it.

When she opened the door, she saw Sloane first, looking like someone had died all over again. Lina towered over her, somehow managing to look even more jagged and raw than usual. Maybe it was the fresh tattoo on her left wrist, still swollen and seeping around the edges. Anger radiated off of her in waves but there was something else there too—something Madge couldn't place. Rose hovered in the background, off the front steps near the grass. Maybe she was scared of what would happen now that she'd managed to unite Madge's friends together against her. Or maybe she wanted to avoid the new outsider.

Rose opened her mouth to speak, but Lina beat her to it.

"How could you do that?" she spat.

Madge took a step back.

"Do you realize what could have happened? If one of them died, it would be traced back to you, to *us*. And then what?"

Lina threw her hands in the air, pacing back and forth in the entryway. Her eyes were glassy with tears that would never dare fall in front of them. Madge had never seen her so upset. Not even the night of Willa's death. "I get that the War isn't enough for you, that you're on some sort of suicide mission. If you have a death wish, that's fine. Awesome. But don't drag us down with you. I'm not about to destroy my life for those assholes, and you shouldn't be either. They've already done enough damage."

"I . . . I . . ." Madge began but could formulate no response. For once in her life she had nothing to say. She looked at Rose. She wanted to hate her for reporting back to Sloane and Lina, for giving her up. But she couldn't. She saw nothing but concern in Rose's dark eyes and nothing but disappointment in Sloane's. Still, all she could think about was how she hadn't tried hard enough the previous night, that if she were a little stronger, if she'd had more time, if she'd planned ahead, she could have won. She wondered if this was what James felt like when he reached for another drink. Powerless to stop—

The phone buzzed in her hand, and she dropped it to the wood floor in surprise. It continued vibrating along the planks. At the same time, Sloane's chirped, Lina's rattled in her purse, and Rose's jingled. Madge's eyes widened. It was too much of a coincidence to be a coincidence.

A text had arrived. Caller Unknown. A link to a webpage. Nothing else. As if in a nightmare, the four girls picked up their phones and clicked on the series of numbers and letters.

Lina went pale first, her finger instinctively deleting the message before she even had time to analyze it. When Madge turned her eyes back on her own phone, she saw why. A photo jumped onto her screen: Lina standing next to a girl Madge recognized as a bartender from the Club, her hand draped lazily over Lina's shoulder. Their faces were a whisper apart, the girl's teeth seemingly biting Lina's ear.

Coupled with the shocking image were five simple words.

Is she or isn't she?

Another photo appeared. This time Sloane's eyes went wide, her chest rising and falling with rapid breaths as though she were about to hyperventilate. On the screen was a picture of a sheet of paper, PSAT test results typed at the top, certain lines highlighted in glaring yellow.

28 Critical Reading

22 Mathematics

33 Writing Skills

10th percentile

I thought all Asians were smart?

The slideshow continued.

Or maybe she's just street smart.

The shot was blurry, but clearly showed Sloane handing something to Rory O'Neil, the stoner from Lina's pictures. Either she was buying drugs or selling them, but as tears slipped down her cheeks and she crouched to the floor shaking, the difference didn't matter.

Sloane threw her phone to the ground like it was a hand grenade.

Madge held her breath. Rose was next. Not that it offered Madge much comfort.

This photo was of the Captain's hands beneath a woman's dress, her hair dark and wild, her skin rich like her daughter's. If Madge didn't know better, she'd wonder if it was Rose in the picture, her face lifted to the ceiling in ecstasy.

The detective's wife has a hobby.

Madge thought she might be sick. She was next. She wanted to be alone for it, to witness whatever it was in solitude so she could wrap her head around it, process the destruction by herself. And retaliate.

"What's happening?" Lina whispered through her hand clamped over her lips. "Sloane, what is this? That's the guy who supplies the Gregorys with pills . . ." She held her phone up with the picture of Sloane and the druggie.

Sloane shook her head defensively, crying uncontrollably. She held her own phone out to Lina. "Why didn't you tell me? I'm your best friend."

Scarlet spread across Lina's face and she deflected Sloane's question by turning to Rose, her eyes like daggers. "It's true? This is why you wanted in? To protect your slut of a mother? Because—"

"SHUT UP!" Madge yelled. "Everybody inside."

Without a word, they followed her into the hall. She slammed the front door behind them. Her hand shook as she looked down at the screen. She felt her stomach drop out from under her as she read the words on the screen. There was no picture on this last slide.

You killed her, Madge. I have proof.

"It's you, isn't it?" Lina choked on the words.

"What?"

"You sent out this slideshow. Is this all part of some twisted plan to keep us in the War? Are you blackmailing us into fighting?"

Madge collapsed under the weight of the accusation. "No, God no. How could you . . ." She couldn't bring herself to finish her question. How could they think that? How could they not?

"You don't understand. It wasn't . . . I would never . . . Just look." Madge held out her phone. "This is a message for *me*. They saved me for last because I started this!"

"But who else could have gotten these?" Sloane shook her head at her phone as though it held answers instead of an unknown number. Her forehead twisted under the weight of everything.

"James?" Lina asked, her voice barely audible.

"Not James. Trip." Rose spoke with a quiet authority.

"But I thought James was the one who caught you guys last night," Lina stated.

Madge found she could no longer breathe. She could only watch in horror as her friends, the three people closest to her in the world—yes, even Rose—debated her innocence. For the first time in her life, she truly understood what "powerless" meant.

"No, he was there, too. In the window. He saw everything." Rose looked to Madge, who nodded. She remembered the movement she'd seen in the upstairs window. She remembered the realization she'd had in that moment. She should have known this was coming. Trip was dangerous, much more dangerous than his brother.

Willa's death had been ruled an accident. Trip had made sure to make it look like he'd found James all alone on the boat. Madge knew he was lying. Perhaps she'd always known. But she couldn't say anything without admitting that she'd abandoned her sister out there on the water. She was so mad and so frustrated with Willa that she'd left her there to die. *She* really was a murderer.

Sloane shook her head, as if reading Madge's thoughts. "It was me. I killed Willa."

"What are you talking about Sloane? You weren't even there. I saw . . . I saw things. I know what happened to my sister, and it had nothing to do with you."

"But it was me. Those drugs she took? They were my

stupid narcolepsy pills. The ones my parents prescribed after I passed out and missed curfew. I never took them so I gave them away. I didn't know Rory . . ." She shook her head again, her silky black hair flying around her face. "I'm so sorry, I can't believe. I just can't believe this is all my fault." Sloane covered her eyes and began to shake with silent sobs.

Madge watched as Lina wrapped her arms around their friend. But then, as if something clicked, she slowly pulled her body away and took a step back. She patted Sloane on the shoulder instead, her fingers avoiding the bare flesh of her friend's arm. Madge walked over to Sloane and gently pulled her hands away from her face. She took Sloane's hands into her own. "This isn't your fault. I saw James drive the boat away. And I trusted Trip. For some messed up reason, I trusted a Gregory."

Rose twisted the key around her neck. Everyone listened as Madge continued.

"He said he saw her, he said he saw my sister get on that boat." Her voice broke a little when she imagined Willa lying there, blonde hair pooled and sparkling in the moonlight. "But when he came back, she was gone. I don't know why, I don't know how, but they did this. Don't you dare blame yourself."

Then she turned to Lina. "And *you*. I love you. Even if your taste in women is awful." Lina's eyes filled with tears and she looked down at her hands. "And you know I hate huggers, but for you, I'll make an exception." She wrapped her arms around her friend tightly and kissed her on the cheek.

"And Rose, your mom is awful. She and my stepmother would get along famously, and that is *so* not a compliment." Madge grabbed Rose's hand and squeezed. "You're one of us now, whether you . . ."

A sharp pounding on the front door cut her off. Madge's shaky smile melted. Her words dripped away. This was it. The end. It was all happening exactly the way it did on TV. The police were here to arrest her for her sister's death, and she had no evidence of what really happened. No proof of her innocence. It was just her word against Trip Gregory's and at the Club, what he said would always trump what she said. She swung open the door to find a courier in a neatly pressed uniform with a small box.

"Ms. Ames-Rowan?"

Madge could only nod.

"Please sign here."

She moved the stylus across the machine without even trying to sign her name. "There's no return address," she said nodding toward the mysterious package.

"The sender wishes to remain anonymous." He handed her the box and winked.

It was such a simple gesture, might have even seemed friendly under different circumstances, but the wink made her want to be sick. There was something bad in that box. Something evil. Maybe even deadly. She reluctantly hurried to the living room and placed it on the coffee table. The girls followed.

"Well?" Rose cocked an eyebrow.

"I can't open it." Madge shook her head. "I can't do it."

"Once you open it, you can't close it," Sloane said.

Madge thought for a second how true that really was. How now that they'd started the War none of this could be closed again. Not the way it used to be.

"Enough of this already." Lina grabbed the package and tore it open. When she pulled out a small velvet jewelry box, Madge gasped out loud. She recognized the powder blue. She and Willa had each gotten one the day her dad married Carol. It had contained a tiny gold necklace with a knot that was supposed to symbolize their new family ties or some bullshit like that. Madge had told her father that he should have made them golden nooses. He was not amused. But Willa had loved hers. She'd sighed over the pristine corners of the blue box with its white block lettering, and she'd let out a little squeal when she saw the dainty necklace. "I'll never take it off," she'd whispered. And as far as Madge knew, she'd stayed true to her word.

Lina slowly pulled the necklace out of the box. There was a small card attached like a tag.

"Is that . . ." Sloane couldn't bring herself to finish.

Madge reached for the slip of paper.

You have twenty-four hours to surrender before I tell the police that I saw you kill Willa. I have the evidence to put you in jail. I saved this for you. Something to remember her by.

Lina examined the clasp. "You guys, this is broken, like someone . . ." she took a breath as her eyes filled with tears. "Like someone ripped it off her neck."

Madge turned on her heel and walked upstairs to her room.

"What the hell? Where are you going?" Lina yelled up after her.

"I'm getting dressed. We're going to the bank." She threw on a sundress and twisted her hair into a ponytail. She was done with all this cloak-and-dagger bullshit. The time for the final battle had arrived. If it had to be public, then it would be. There was nothing left to lose, so there was nothing left to hide.

Chapter 28

Previous trips to the bank had been carefully orchestrated to avoid calling attention to the fact that four teenage girls were accessing a safety deposit box. But today there wasn't time for theatrics. One girl after the next, they filed into the expansive hall, gathering looks and whispers and skepticism with each step.

Madge slapped the key on the counter in front of the teller.

Eyes followed the girls as the bank manager guided them down the stairs, through the vault and into a private booth. The stark steel box he presented didn't look like much sitting on the laminate counter, but with or without the cash, it was pretty much the most valuable thing Madge owned.

Madge's entire world had come crashing down when her mother was diagnosed with late-stage pancreatic cancer. Like most seven-year-olds, she was a tiny moon who faithfully orbited her mother every day and every night. But suddenly her world was a hospital bed, attached to so many tubes and needles that Madge couldn't recall the *before* without looking at the pictures that lined the side table like a previous life. And just as suddenly there wasn't even a hospital bed to orbit. Madge was at sea in the vast universe with no one to tether her to reality. The goodbye she'd always imagined evaporated with her mother's wish to be remembered alive and not dead. At seven, Madge had been forced to find her closure in a casket. She whispered goodbye as she knelt in front of it but had no real understanding of what her life would look like now that her mother was inside that box.

After the funeral, Madge spent hours in her mother's closet, digging through jewelry boxes and clothes, desperate to find something that she might have left behind for her only daughter. But there was nothing. Just stuff that vaguely smelled like the woman who was already shifting and fading out of focus. Madge's biggest fear was not knowing if she remembered her mom for who she truly was or if she was reconstructing her from those bedside pictures and home videos. She hated her mother for leaving her, she hated her mother for never saying goodbye, she hated her mother for not being stronger. And then, on her thirteenth birthday, her father placed a small, carefully wrapped package on her bed.

It had taken Madge almost a week to work up the courage to open the present. Truth be told, when she finally did, she was underwhelmed. A tiny safety deposit box key lay tucked in a white velvet box. A note written in her mother's careful script explained that the key would open up safety deposit box number 732 at Hawthorne Lake Savings and Trust. The box had been handed down from mother to daughter in her mother's family for nearly three generations. It was a place for a woman to hide her secrets. A place where she could keep her most valuable thoughts and possessions safe from fathers and husbands. It was the moment Madge was finally able to forgive her mother for abandoning her. Because in a way, she never had.

So it was Madge who pulled her long gold chain off her neck and twisted the key in the tiny lock. It was Madge who gasped first when she opened the box to find it empty except for a single hundred dollar bill and a note scratched on a sheet of notebook paper.

"What the hell?" Lina's voice bounced off the marble floors of the booth.

If I managed to get the key, why would I leave the money? Better safe than sorry, girls.

"Now what?" Rose looked like she was going to be sick.

"I could probably get my parents to give us some more money." Sloane twisted her own key thoughtfully.

Lina collapsed into a worn leather club chair. "They've had their fun; we gave it our best shot, I think it's time to call it a day. At least now we can all stop faking it and get on with our lives."

"You're kidding right?" Madge could barely even process Lina's words. "You really think they're just going to leave well enough alone now? That they're not going to do everything in their power to make it look like I killed my sister?" Her chest was tight and her legs went numb. It wouldn't be hard to make her look guilty. She'd been so angry with Willa. She'd said so many awful things. She'd left her on that boat with both Gregorys. Madge's lungs tightened and her chest heaved. No air. There was never enough air. Willa. This was what it must have felt like when she went under. When she couldn't breathe.

"Oh my God, what's wrong with her? What's happening?" Madge heard Sloane's voice but she couldn't see her.

She was too focused on getting air to her lungs to realize that her eyes were squeezed shut.

"I think it's a panic attack. Move back, you guys! She needs to sit down." Rose's voice was insistent.

Arms guided her carefully into a chair and forced her head between her knees. Madge felt the weight of her friends' hands on her shoulders, rubbing her back and holding her hand. They fixed her, pieced most of the broken parts back together. Her lungs opened. This was it. There was no turning back. The money was gone. Madge closed her eyes and let herself swim in the blackness a little longer.

"I know what we can do," she said.

The words were out of her mouth before she could even lift her head from her lap. When she was finally upright and the room settled back into focus, three sets of eyes sized her up.

"You can't be serious. This is over. We've lost everything." Lina's voice was incredulous, her tattooed arms twined together to stave off the chill of the air-conditioned bank.

"Exactly. Listen to yourself. We've lost everything. There's nothing left to lose. They're going to come after me anyway. Now is the time to strike."

"But there's no money." Sloane stared at the empty deposit box.

"We don't need money. We have information." A slow smile twisted Madge's lips. "Does that one guy you're always bitching about still do web design? Jude What's-his-Face?"

"Uh, yeah, but I don't think it's a good . . ."

"Call him." Madge sat straighter, tugging at the key around her neck.

"But are you sure? I mean he's kind of—"

"Call." Madge held out her cell phone to Sloane. Rose and Lina leaned in, softening.

"But we only have a hundred dollars, and I'm sure it costs way more . . ." Sloane looked around the walls of the bank desperately searching for some kind of out.

"Call!" This time the voices of all three girls rang out in unison.

Sloane stared at them for a minute and started to giggle. It was so unexpected. So out of place in the stodgy bowels of the bank that Madge felt a laugh bubble up in her throat. Pretty soon they were all at it. A tear-streaming, stomach-aching kind of laughter echoing off the close walls.

"Everything okay in here, ladies?" The bank manager knocked on the door to their tiny room, but none of them could pull themselves together enough to respond.

Madge knew it was hysteria, gallows humor, but it was laughter all the same. Madge couldn't remember the last time it had felt this good.

Chapter 29

When it came to Sloane, Jude Yang always said yes. Madge reminded herself of this as she paced the attic floors. Sloane occupied her normal seat by the window, forehead meeting the glass. Lina's legs were pulled to her chest, her cheek resting on a knee. Rose sat ramrod straight in a chair, her crossed leg shaking rhythmically.

When he knocked, everyone stopped. Madge rushed to the door, but Sloane beat her to it, placing a hand on her shoulder. "I'll open it."

Jude was bathed in Yale paraphernalia as usual, his computer bag slung across his body. Madge started talking the second he set foot in the room, taking him through every step of the plan and swearing him to secrecy. He stared at Sloane the whole time, the way he always did, with a mixture of clumsiness and infatuation. Madge knew then that secrecy was a given, that they had this in the bag. She fought back hope, though. Hope was too dangerous. Better to cling to desperation.

"Let's do this," he said simply.

For the next several hours, the girls hovered over the screen as he typed mysterious codes into his computer and asked questions about color, font, and format. Lina emailed Jude the pictures she'd gathered from social sites, or scanned from the pages of the yearbooks and newspapers that were still stacked in the corner. The website began to take shape and chronicled the sordid true story of the Gregory brothers. James naked on the beach. Videos of drug deals. Close-up stills of tiny white pills. They dug up photos from the boys' casino parties, stacks of money, and hordes of alcohol. Violet Garretson's picture was uploaded as well, along with a statement she'd sent Madge in response to an email about her experience with James and her subsequent exile from the Club. But most importantly: Willa. Her picture and their first-hand accounts of what transpired on July Fourth all told Willa's story with unflinching honesty. Their War published on the Internet, for the world to see.

"You sure about this?" Jude shifted in the uncomfortable chair to acknowledge each of the girls. He looked greenish. Madge couldn't blame him. It was a lot to swallow.

Three heads bobbed up and down. Not Madge's. Hers shook.

"Wait, it's missing something." Her lips pursed as she thought. "We need a comments section. A place where girls can tell their own story. For every Willa, there's a Nadia or a Kira. They all deserve to be heard."

Jude nodded. "Easy enough." He typed into the keyboard for a couple of minutes and then turned back around. "Good?"

"Good." The girls echoed.

He hit one key with a final flourish.

. . .

As they exited the attic, pushing open the great painting that hid the space, noon light spilled into the parlor in bright stripes. Jude refused to take the remaining hundred dollars. He said he couldn't "in good conscience," given what he now knew. He flushed when Sloane swept him up in an awkward hug, then he hurried off. Madge wondered if he'd ever come back to the Club again.

Rose steered everyone down one of the winding hallways toward her mother's office, but Madge hung back a step. Her finger trailed the wall, almost as if to anchor herself to it. She knew in a matter of moments, her life would change once again.

No matter how many times she told herself that starting the War wasn't going to bring back her sister, she still saw Willa swimming up to that sandbar. She would grab Madge's hand and apologize for not holding it during the fireworks, for taking so long. Madge would let herself cry then, sobs wracking her thin shoulders at what could have been. But as she stared down the hall at her friends it was as though someone had flipped a switch forcing her to squint through the harsh light of reality. All at once, she knew Willa wasn't coming home. She could wait forever, punish herself, fight, but Willa was gone. She had to let her sister go.

The door to Mrs. McCaan's office was closed, but Rose didn't bother knocking, she just threw it open and stormed right inside.

The office was empty.

"Mom?" The word echoed against the dusty walls. "Okay, we're good." Rose flipped the laptop open and pulled up her mom's email system and selected the mailing list for the entire

Club. With trembling fingers she typed in the web address www.thisiswar.com and hit send.

It was done.

Madge was the first one to leave. The girls followed behind, their footsteps silent on the padded carpets that lined the Club's halls. She led them outside, past the pool and then farther onto the beach. As she made her way closer to the edge of the water, she kicked off her shoes—the sand smooth on her feet, the water tickling her toes. The girls did the same. She sat close enough to the water's edge that the tiny waves lapped at her feet. She closed her eyes and tilted her face toward the sun. The heat felt good on Madge's cheeks, but the weight of Lina's head on her shoulder felt even better.

"For Willa," Madge whispered.

"For Willa," Lina echoed.

It didn't take long.

By the time the girls had returned to the Club pool, there were over 100 comments on the site. (The pool was also conspicuously deserted.) All were from girls who had been abused, disenfranchised, or otherwise maligned by the Gregory family. Madge didn't bother going home. She knew it was useless to hide. Instead she dangled her feet into the water and read the comments one by one, trying to guess who they belonged to. The girls sat behind her, sprawled out on various lawn chairs. Sloane snored softly while Rose kept checking her phone, no doubt waiting for the axe to fall from her mother. Lina followed the stories on her phone, reading the particularly scandalous entries out loud for everyone's benefit.

Madge tried to savor what felt like a carefree moment. It wouldn't last. Nothing did.

When she felt a shadow chill her skin, she knew it was over.

"Ms. Ames-Rowan, I'm afraid there's a rather pressing issue we need to address in my office. Immediately. Do you mind?" The Captain's rough hand gripped Madge's bare shoulder. He glanced at the other girls, but there was no question in his eyes, only command. Madge nodded at her friends. The girls stood silently and departed, leaving Madge trapped beneath his calloused fingers. True, she didn't expect them to put up a fight right then and there. She couldn't help but feel abandoned. Then again, maybe she deserved it.

The Captain ushered her toward the massive mahogany doors of his office. She had no idea what lay behind them, but it didn't matter anymore. Yes, Madge and her friends had lost the War. But with the birth of the website, Madge hoped the Gregorys couldn't hurt anyone anymore. The Captain pulled the door open and Madge took one hesitant step inside. There, waiting in antique club chairs so old that the leather cracked and peeled around the edges was Trip Gregory, Detective McCaan, Carol, and her father. Madge felt her knees buckle as the Captain closed the doors. But it was the sight of Willa's phone on his desk that finally sent her tumbling to the floor.

Chapter 30

All Madge could remember about the previous day were eyes.

The Captain's were sharp and predatory, flicking around the room in search of a target, his aim impeccable. When they landed, it burned. Detective McCaan's were tinged pink and puffy as though he'd been crying or hadn't slept for weeks. He rubbed them repeatedly, which only seemed to make things worse, the corners pulled down in perpetual worry. Trip's were a watery blue, the most attractive thing about him if you could ignore the way they sized you up, falling in all the wrong places. And from what she could see of her father's and Carol's, they were vacant, cloudy, unseeing. Of course much of that was speculation. They could barely look at her.

And now she was locked in the house. Whispers trailed down the hall from her parents' bedroom and slipped beneath the crack of her door like ghosts.

"You saw the phone. The messages she sent to Willa. They found her out on that sandbar. Maybe that's why they wanted us to stop the investigation. They must have known . . ."

So strange how Madge hadn't regretted typing that text to Willa at the time. She'd wanted to say something even worse as her sister sped away with James. The anger had tasted bitter on her tongue. *i'm gonna kill u. i mean it.* Those words were the last she'd communicated to Willa. That is, if you didn't count the way she screamed her name over and over again from the sandbar, eyes wild and burning as they searched the endless black.

Trip claimed to have turned it in after supposedly finding it on the yacht earlier that week. His face was apologetic, but Madge saw the thin sheen of satisfaction in his eyes. The phone was his trump card. He must have been sitting on it the whole time, waiting for the perfect moment to play it. And now, he'd finally slapped it down on the table and won.

"She's not well, Carol. She's found a way to deflect the blame. That website is in direct violation of our agreement. We have to talk to him . . ."

Smoke seemed to drift through the vents and from beneath the sill of the window, through cracks in the floor, billowing around her like a cloud. She thought of the revolution she'd hoped to start, of that first meeting, lighting candles, planning, then blowing them out, trails of smoke urging the girls onward. Her dad was right. She wasn't well. Maybe she deserved to be punished. Maybe they all did.

"You heard the detective. They'll reopen the case. She'd be a suspect, David."

Surely now was the time to give up. It would be easier to hold her hands in the air, palms up, and surrender. She thought of Willa all alone in the water, struggling to stay afloat even though she'd been drugged. Or maybe there wasn't a struggle. Maybe her sister had fallen into the water and sunk to the bottom like a stone. Maybe she'd let the water wrap slippery fingers around her neck and tug the life right out of her. Maybe it was time for Madge to follow in her footsteps.

But then the door to her room cracked open, and Madge sat up in her bed a bit straighter. Lina poked her blonde head in, a finger poised at her lips. *Shhh.*

For that brief second before anyone slipped in, Madge swore she saw Willa in the empty space. A ghost or maybe just a trick of the light. Either way, she tasted mint and smelled ashes. Sloane and Rose slipped through the gap where Willa should have been, and Lina gently shut the door. All of her friends approached her on the bed, taking her hands in theirs, no one uttering a word. The silence was striking, their tear-filled eyes catching on one another. Madge thought they were lost to her, these friends. They'd surrendered her so easily yesterday, and she didn't blame them. Not really. But she'd been wrong. The relief was almost sweet enough to overcome the sickly taste in her mouth. Almost.

"There's not a lot of time," Rose whispered, breaking the spell. "When the Captain took you, we went to James." She lowered her head, trying to hide how she felt about the boy. Madge couldn't imagine how hard it must have been for her to go to him. "He wants to make this right."

Sloane wiped beneath her eyes. Everyone had always known James killed Willa, but no one was prepared for how the truth would feel when proven. And no matter what, they each felt their own sense of responsibility, their own hand in Willa's death. They always would.

"He promised to go to the Captain. To turn himself in," Lina broke in. "He promised to end this."

Sloane reached into her bag and pulled out a phone, laying it gently in the center of Madge's bed. Madge wrinkled her forehead in confusion. She'd never seen it before. "We gave this to Nadia so we could record James's confession. It should all be on here." Sloane's dark eyes pierced Madge's and hope swirled within her. She felt dizzy with the power of it. Even though she knew it was dangerous, she couldn't help herself. Could it be? Was the War really not lost? They had the truth. On tape . . .

Rose nudged the phone toward Madge. "We waited for you. It didn't seem fair to listen without you."

Lina threw Madge a jagged smile. Madge brought the phone to life, her fingers shaking as she slid them across the screen to access the recording.

The girls leaned closer into the circle, into position. Madge pressed play.

They heard movement first, shifting bodies, shuffling papers. And then James's voice, strong and clear.

"You have to stop this. Madge didn't kill Willa and you know it. I killed her, Grandpa. Everyone knows."

Static crackled through the speaker and the next sound caused goose bumps to erupt, trailing along Madge's arms and legs. The Captain laughed. Madge dug her fingernails into the palms of her hands, willing them to break skin. How could he laugh?

"You really believe that, don't you?"

Silence from James.

"You didn't kill that girl, James. Trip did. And the boy couldn't even manage not to screw that up, worthless son of a bitch. He set it up to look like it was you. You know what happened with your parents. You know he never recovered from me cutting him out of the will. He's sick, James. Your brother is sick and now we're paying for it."

The girls jumped when his fist slammed on top of the desk.

"Do you know how much money I had to pay that girl's

parents to keep this whole thing quiet to preserve our family's name? To keep the Club out of the national news?"

Madge felt her stomach heave. The money. The sudden improvement in their finances. The conversation she'd over-heard in her dad's office. How could she have missed this? She looked around her room, at the clothes in her closet, the shoes strewn on the floor. How much of it had been pur-chased after Willa died? How much of her sister's blood did she have on her own hands?

"I've got an entire team of people working to get that site down, but it's protected by more firewalls than the CIA. The damn thing refuses to die. Thank God your idiot brother at least had the foresight to set up that Madge Ames-Rowan. Serves her right."

Madge's eyes grew wide, and she pushed her shaking fin-gers against her lips not knowing what else to do with them. The recording crackled as the girls leaned closer, afraid they might miss something. But the silence continued.

"No."

From James.

It was a wonder she'd even caught it, a wonder anyone did. The word barely registered on the recorder. Madge tried to imagine what the Captain might look like if he'd heard the word slip out of James's mouth. She didn't have time to find out. They had heard enough. Madge fumbled with the phone, her body shaking violently. Everyone's eyes were wide, jaws slack, frozen.

"We have to go. We have to go NOW." Madge jumped up and shot for the door.

Little waves of heat radiated off the sidewalk leading into the squat brown building that housed Hawthorne Lake's tiny police station. This was Rose's turf, so Madge dutifully fell in line behind her. One by one, the girls marched through the front door, straight past the front desk and toward Detective McCaan's office.

"Wait! Rose! You can't go in there. He's with . . ." The plump woman in uniform at reception was flushed and panicked, but none of the girls even turned to look at her. They were on a mission and nothing was going to stop them. Least of all Madge, who finally held the truth, quite literally, in the palm of her hands.

"Look, there's just no evidence. It's your word against his and the autopsy results came back—" Detective McCaan stopped mid-sentence as the girls filed into his office. James Gregory sat across from him, gaping at the small but determined army before him.

"We have evidence." Rose looked at her father with a mixture of pity and hope.

Just as Madge's finger hovered over the play button on the screen, the Captain barreled in.

"Stop!" he bellowed.

Madge froze not because she wanted to, but because her body was somehow still unable to disobey the authority in the Captain's tone.

"I need five minutes with Ms. Ames-Rowan," he said easing himself into the chair at the head of the table.

"I really can't have you in here right now, sir." Detective McCaan's voice was soft, pleading.

"I'm not asking, I'm telling. I need her alone. Five minutes. Go!"

"I'll be fine," Madge nodded at the girls, Detective McCaan, and finally James, who shook his head, eyes wide. Madge waited and took his chair. James hesitated but finally walked out of the office. The others followed.

Detective McCaan was last. "I'll be right outside if you need me," he said, with a sharp eye at the Captain.

The finality of the door's click was fitting.

"This stops here," he said evenly. His blue eyes pierced her own. "I need you to give me that recording and take down that damn website."

Madge did her best to choke back a snort. "Yeah, sure. I'll get right on that."

"Two million dollars." The Captain leaned forward in his seat. "The first payment to your parents was five million. The money will transfer semi-anually for the next five years. But you must agree to my terms."

"What would possibly lead you to believe that I'd choose money over justice?" Madge's hand flew to the key around her neck. A reminder of what was at stake.

"You'll have justice, too. Trip will be tried as an adult, for one. He deserves to be. I have evidence that demonstrates this was premeditated. If he's tried as an adult, he'll get life in jail. Maybe even the death sentence." The Captain leaned back in his chair and crossed his legs. His jaw twitched. "The attorney general won't touch him without my blessing, so I'll ensure he gets prosecuted to the fullest extent of the law. It's justice. Besides, justice is what Willa would have wanted."

Madge was already up and out of her seat. "You don't get to say her name. Not ever." Her palms slapped the wood desk.

"Punishing me, destroying the Club, that won't bring her back, Madge. But making sure her mother is well taken care of, providing financial stability for your family, those are things that were very important to your sister."

The Captain stood and reached past Madge to open the door for her. "Of course I know you want to do the *right* thing, in which case I will update the terms of my agreement with your father and begin the repayment process. Just say the word." He raised an eyebrow, challenging her.

He might as well have pushed her head under water. She had no choice. She never had any choice.

Madge hesitated, overcome by memories. Willa's smile over cereal in the morning, screaming for Madge to hurry up in the shower, tearing out of the house when their homework was finally done, text messages, shopping trips, whispers in their beds, late-night swimming, trick-or-treating, Christmas. Everything rushed in at once, pressing down on her, shoving her back under.

"He's sick, Madge. My grandson is sick, and your sister is dead. Nothing can bring her back, but you have my word that Trip will pay."

Madge straightened her body to stand at full height in front of the Captain. "I'll take the website down." And she turned before she could see his satisfied smile. She raced through the police station, avoiding her friends' and the Detective's eyes. She pushed through the door and collapsed onto the sidewalk in front. Fire burned in her throat. No matter how hard she tried to swallow them back, tears followed. They streamed down her cheeks, hung on her jaw for a second and exploded onto the cement below. Had she done the right thing? What would Willa have done? As much as she hated to admit it, the Captain was right. Willa would have wanted Trip to pay for killing her. Not James. Not her friends. Not anyone else.

And the Captain? Well, someone else would have to solve that problem.

Madge was done.

"She deserved someone better than me." James spoke

behind her but Madge didn't dare turn for fear of display-
ing her tear-stained cheeks. "I never could have been good
enough."

Madge knew exactly what he meant, had spoken the same
words to Willa in the dead of the night, curled in on herself
between her sister's empty sheets. Willa deserved a better sister, one who wouldn't have left her behind.

"She was so lucky though. She was lucky to have you."

She shook her head. Even though she didn't believe him,
wasn't sure she ever would, she lifted her face to the sun and
turned to meet his broken eyes. "You did the right thing," she
whispered.

This time James had to turn away, his back to her, head
bowed. After a minute, he walked to a car where a friend was
waiting and ducked into the passenger seat. She wasn't the
only one with a long road ahead.

And then one by one, shadows appeared over her. Three
angelic forms, silhouetted in the sun. Her friends. At least she
wasn't going to have to go through any of it alone.

Chapter 31

Madge stood in front of the dusty attic window tracing her fingers along what had to be Sloane's handprints, watching for her friends. It'd been over a month since one of the valets had driven Trip's expensive car off the property and over to the used car lot in the center of town. Like so many others, Trip had simply disappeared from Hawthorne Lake, never to be heard from again. Unlike the others, however, his picture was everywhere. The Captain had spent long hours talking in soothing tones about the moment he'd discovered his grandson was guilty of murder—the importance of equality and justice in a world where the rich were rarely held accountable for their crimes. The Captain was a local hero and Willa was Hawthorne Lake's sweetheart. In that way, things were very much the same.

Madge was trying to force herself to forget because she knew she'd never, ever be able to forgive. But the anger was still there. Black and terrible. She did her best to keep it at bay because Willa wouldn't have wanted her to be angry or sad.

Willa would have wanted her to move on, to live her life, to find pockets of happiness and hope.

So Madge spent her days trying to avoid the news, where Willa's beautiful blonde picture and the Captain's sound-bytes were in heavy rotation. She holed up at the Club with her friends. The Captain had pumped up security to protect her family from the media. At least that's what he'd said in interviews.

Of course, every time she returned home, she was reminded that everything had been paid for in her sister's blood. She'd have to learn to live with that, too . . .

Jude Yang's car pulled up the drive, and Sloane climbed out. She leaned into the window and said goodbye. Even from the distance, Madge saw his face light up. The two had been spending more time together. Even though he was headed back to school in a couple weeks, Madge knew something had sparked. Lina called out to Sloane, and Madge watched her jog over. The girls laughed together and turned toward the entrance, where they bumped into Rose and James. He squeezed her hand for a beat before hurrying off.

It was hard for Madge to watch Rose and James together. Hard to watch him falling in love after all the years he spent ignoring her sister. But he was entitled to some happiness. He was back in rehab, seeing a therapist, doing community service—not because he had to, but because he'd volunteered. He spent far less time at the Club than in the past. Another sign that Willa Ames-Rowan and James Gregory were never meant to be together. James had pined for Rose long before Willa had died. Probably long before Willa had even developed a crush on him. She wondered how long it would have taken Willa to realize that she didn't have to be with someone like James just because it was expected or convenient or profitable. She should have had the chance to figure it out.

Madge listened for her friends' footsteps on the wood stairs.

"Creeper! Were you spying on us?" Lina pushed open the door to the attic and laughed at Madge, still perched at the window.

"Bird's eye view." Madge raised her eyebrows.

Sloane threw herself into the old couch. "I can't believe you're leaving for school tomorrow, Lina. Why can't you stay around here like the rest of us?"

Lina snorted. "Yeah right. You think my parents could wait until college to get rid of me?"

Madge knew the housekeeper had probably spent the last week packing her up for boarding school just like all the other years.

"We'll be okay, though, right?" Rose asked.

Madge considered her question and wondered what it really meant to be okay. Had she ever been okay? Would she ever be okay? She'd finally removed Willa's flip-flops from under her bed. Did that mean anything?

"Better than okay, we'll be fabulous," she said at last. Even if she wasn't sure it was true, it was exactly what Willa would have said. It felt good to borrow one of her lines.

Just then her phone buzzed. In a fleeting instant of forget-fulness and habit, she wondered if it was her sister calling to yell at the girls for not waiting for her or to ask Madge if she could borrow her turquoise necklace or warn her that Carol was pissed again. But then she remembered.

That habit would be hard to break.

When she looked down, she had a new text from an unknown number. Her heart raced. It was the kind of text that you knew not to open, Spam or a virus or something that would otherwise destroy your phone: a single link, like the one Trip had sent. But it didn't take long for Madge to recognize the address.

www.thisiswar.com

And one by one, the other girls' phones sounded and buzzed. Their foreheads wrinkled in confusion.

"I thought Jude took this down, right Sloane?" Lina asked.

Before she could stop herself, Madge clicked the link, her heart pounding now. When the website came into view, it looked different. Madge released the air she'd trapped in her lungs. *Thank God.*

"Someone else stole our site," Rose said.

"But . . ." Sloane turned her phone toward the girls. There were 10,541 comments. Madge narrowed her eyes and took the phone, clicking the newest comment. It featured another link, and before clicking, she looked up. All the girls nodded. When she clicked, the browser took them to some town's local paper and a short article appeared on the screen with an accompanying picture.

Boy Accused of Date Rape Faces Vigilante Justice

The picture was blurry, obviously taken with a phone. A boy around their age was bound to a telephone pole at a busy intersection in New Haven, Connecticut. It wasn't the fact that he was completely naked aside from a lacy bra and boxer shorts that made Madge drop her phone. It was the acronym that had been scrawled across his chest in thick black marker.

W.A.R.

July 4th, 11:21 P.M.

Willa regretted getting in the boat with James almost as soon as he'd gunned the motor, heading toward the sandbar in the middle of the lake at breakneck speed. The boat crashed against the water, making her head spin and her eyes blur. She was tired but she didn't want to fall asleep. Not when she was finally alone with James Gregory. Even though something inside her resisted the turn of the night, something screamed at her to be careful, she was still with James. She might as well make the most of it.

When he turned off the engine, Willa knew this was her chance. Her moment. She slid closer to him, closed her eyes and went in for the kiss.

"Rose . . ." he mumbled.

"What the hell?" She felt a surge of rage. But still, she was not nearly as surprised as she could have been. She saw how James's eyes had scanned the crowd for the strange girl, saw the hurt on his face when she slipped away out of his reach.

Willa's eyes grew heavy as she remembered. The rage faded. The truth was she was too tired to feel anything. So tired. That stupid pill Trip had given her must have had something awful in it.

She slumped down on the cushioned bench of the boat and finally let her eyes shut. A warmth spread over her. It had never felt so good to sleep.

She didn't open her eyes again until she felt the boat rock slightly and heard the motor of another boat idling in the background. James was slumped over at the other end, his chest rising with shallow breaths. Even though he was sleeping, she was relieved to see she wasn't alone.

". . . Take it slow. It's dark . . ."

She recognized Trip's voice and heard her sister call back asking if it was okay. Typical Madge, always worrying. Willa felt a quick pang of regret. She shouldn't have bolted like that. That was stupid. Madge was probably ready to kill her. She opened her mouth to call out but couldn't form the words. She could barely move her lips.

"Willa? Willa? You awake?" Trip shook her gently and stroked her cheek. "I'm sorry for this."

Instinct told her to play dead even though there was nothing she wanted more than to dive into the cool water and grasp her sister's hand for help onto her boat. She'd smile brightly and force Madge to return it. A truce. The fireworks were about to start and they always watched together. But Trip scared her then. He was always so playful and fun, never taking himself or life seriously. But his words didn't sound like a joke.

"What about you, James? Ready to know how it feels to be guilty?" Willa heard the dull thud of foot meeting stomach. "Too sleepy, huh? You're welcome for that special

cocktail I whipped up after I had some fun with Rose. Shame you guys never got to see each other tonight." Trip laughed at his own joke.

Willa heard him make his way back to her end of the boat. And then she knew to scream. She lifted her head as much as she could, struggled to prop herself up on her elbows. The world spun when she opened her eyes, but she knew she had to open them. She needed help.

"MA . . ." Only the first part of her sister's name escaped her mouth before his strong fingers clamped over her lips. She felt one arm circle around her waist as he continued to seal her mouth shut with the other. His muscles bulged as he lifted her. As hard as she tried to bite down on his fingers, she couldn't even open her lips. Screams were muffled, barely audible over the lapping of the water—not to mention the fireworks that lit the sky above her. All she could think about was that she was supposed to be with Madge. If only she'd left with Madge.

He released his hand from her mouth, her eyes wildly searching his for a split second before he dumped her body into the lake. Cold, black lake water closed over her. What the hell did he think he was doing? This wasn't funny. But her head was still cloudy, and her arms and legs weren't cooperating when she told them to kick, swim, do anything.

And for a while there was only the darkness and her sick sense of regret. How could she have let this happen? How could she have left Madge and her friends for some stupid guy who was in love with someone else? God, she probably deserved to drown for being such a complete idiot. She pulled at the murky water, her instincts kicking in for a beat, but she was so tired and confused. The night made the lake thick like tar. She lost track of the surface. It would be so easy to stop fighting.

But then she thought of Madge standing on the edge of the boat, screaming her name, and she stopped kicking for a moment, let her body hang in the water so she could feel the upward pull. As soon as she felt the tug, she clawed her way up. Because Willa knew that the brave thing to do was to fight.

It was always tempting to give up and let go, like covering your eyes during the scary part of a movie.

Sometimes it was easier to choose death over life, but it was so much more extraordinary to stare down tragedy and decide to survive. That's where the real story started.

And floating on her back in the darkness of Hawthorne Lake, fireworks exploding overhead and scattering through the sky like rain, Willa chose to live. Willa chose extraordinary. She had never once closed her eyes during a scary movie, and she wasn't about to start now. Life was just getting interesting, and Willa didn't want to miss a thing.

Acknowledgments

This book would not exist without the incomparable Dan "Dam" Ehrenhaft. He earned honorary Roecker sister status when we had to go back and check if he added one of the best lines in the book. (He totally did.)

If you're reading this book it's probably because Meredith Barnes (indirectly) told you to. She's pretty much the best publicist on the planet and earned her honorary (cooler, younger, smarter, New York-ier) Roecker stripes when she sent to-do lists that made Lisa weep with joy.

To the rest of the team at Soho Press for putting so much time, energy and love into our work: Bronwen Hruska, Janine Agro, Rachel Kowal, Paul Oliver, Rudy Martinez, and Amara Hoshijo.

And an extra special thanks to our WriteOnCon cohort, Dustin Hansen, for creating five (!) gorgeous book trailers with zero budget and far too little time.

A huge thanks, as always, to our brilliant literary agent, Catherine Drayton. We'd be lost (and super bored) without her.

And to our husbands/children/parents/in-laws/friends/Romans /countrymen—the only thing more challenging than actually trying to be a writer is being married/related/sired/friends/ acquaintances with a writer. You rock. Thank you for everything.